THE COAL BEGGAR MAID'S CHRISTMAS

VICTORIAN ROMANCE

JESSICA WEIR

PUREREAD.COM

CONTENTS

DEAR READER, GET READY FOR ANOTHER GREAT STORY...

A VICTORIAN ROMANCE

Turn the page and let's begin

CHAPTER 1

"Don't cry my sweetling," Susanne Wilshire said as she lay on death's door, her breathing growing increasingly laboured as she lay upon the bed that she had shared with her husband for eight long years. The physician had done all he could, but it was only a matter of time now. "I'm bound for the Lord's kingdom now, Meg; Mommy isn't going to feel any more pain, so you don't have to keep worrying about me." A tear dropped down the pale blonde's cheek, tracing along the slight cheekbones before falling to the sheet covering her. She gazed into the eyes of her beloved daughter, the eight-year-old a spitting image of her mother.

"Mama, you can't go to God yet. I still need you here! It's Christmas time, and you haven't opened any presents yet." Tears filled the emerald green eyes of the young girl sitting on the edge of the bed, her hands enclosed gently around Susanne's own pale ones.

"You can have my presents, little one." Susanne said sweetly.

"I don't think so... Papa wouldn't be very happy about that." Margaret's little body jerked with a thought. "You can't leave me here alone with just Papa. Papa hates me now, and all he does is hit me."

"Papa doesn't hate you, my sweet. His life is just not going the way he hoped, and he is lost. He knows that my sickness was caused by the coal residue on his clothing from working in the mines. I am sure a part of him will never forgive himself for it. He will need you when I am gone more than you could possibly know. I need to know that I can trust you to help Papa find his way back," Susanne coughed then, grabbing the small handkerchief that her husband had bought her for their eighth anniversary she used it to cover her mouth.

Meg's small pink bottom lip trembled then, her breath coming in quick gasps as she did her best to hold back her sobs. Her hand rubbed across the angular birthmark that marked her right cheek as she angrily brushed away tears. "There are so many things we still have left to do, Mama. You promised that you would be here together with me. You promised!"

"I'm so sorry, my love. I leave you with my blessing. Though my death will be hard on you, I pray that your life is not filled with hardships you cannot bear. Though you may have to suffer for a while, and work harder than most, life will get better for you. That is my final prayer for you," Suzanne whispered, taking one last deep breath before she grew still and spoke no more. The clock chimed midnight as Margaret enter Christmas day all alone.

Ten years later

Margaret Wilshire awoke with tears running down her cheeks. It was cold. Curling up on the thin cot that served as her bed, she pulled her thin blanket to her face to wipe away her tears. Icy tendrils of air came from the window. Forcing themselves through the sizable hole her father had made with an ill-aimed liquor bottle. Margaret moved to one side avoiding the worst of the draft. Still it caught her and left her shivering as she huddled miserably on her cot.

She stretched slowly and deliberately, her once clean golden hair now hanging in tangled knots around her shoulders. It had been a while since she had enjoyed the luxury of soap, having to content herself with wiping down with a washcloth dipped in a pot of cold water. If she was lucky, she would make enough money to buy a small piece from the neighborhood apothecary while panhandling later.

The inconsistent deep breathing and guttural snoring that echoed from the bed to her right told her that her father was still asleep. She was safe for now. A few moments later and she was dreaming again. Only this time she saw the man who had once lovingly hoisted her on his shoulders. Excitement had filled her as she peered over the crowd, her papa towering over everyone in their vicinity.

They had looked so nice dressed in their very best, having taken hours to prepare for the long-anticipated jubilee. It was the 20th of June 1887 and she had the best view of all, feeling safe with her father's strong grip resting comfortably on her legs as she towered over the crowd. The air was filled with the voices of the assembled onlookers ringing out as the colonial forces slowly rode into view astride their noble snorting steeds of brown and black.

Margaret squealed in joy, tugging on her mother's sleeve as she gestured wildly in the direction of the carriage that could only have been the Queen's. Eight cream-colored horses chomped at their bits, whinnying as their muscles bunched with the strain of pulling the massive carriage along the cobbled streets.

The small woman dressed in black immediately drew Margaret's gaze, the woman was dwarfed by the carriage that surrounded her. There was a faint smile on her face as she waved to the various members of the crowd through the window of the carriage, but Margaret thought she could see the familiar lines of sadness that marred the Queen's expression. As she looked closer, the queen began to look more and more like her mother. Their eyes met for the briefest moment, excitement leaping into Margaret's throat as she watched the queen wave. *She's waving at me, isn't she?*

"Meg, get up and go make breakfast," her father said, his voice cutting through the sound of the singing crowd.

Suddenly he was before her in the crowd. No longer the happy, smiling, gentle man but a drunk and a brute. She looked at him in confusion before the world seemed to spin around her. She screamed as she fell through the darkness. Waking, a moment later, she sat bolt upright on her pallet, with sweat dripping down her forehead.

"Did you hear what I said?" A bottle whizzed past her head, sliding through the sizable hole in the bedroom window and shattering against the brick wall that lay below.

She made her way to the kitchen after throwing on her shirtwaist and skirt, to prepare the gruel that served as their usual morning meal. She hesitated about brewing the coffee that her father had won in last Friday's card game, fearing he would be angry with her. He had been out to the tavern later than usual the night before, reeking more of alcohol than was his usual. He had boasted about getting lucky in a game of darts, though Margaret could hardly believe that. He had likely robbed another drunk of his money while they were too inebriated to resist. Not that she would ever voice her suspicions to his face.

Her mind flashed back to her mother, the image of the beautiful golden-haired woman who had been Margaret's personal hero caused her heart to sink in her chest. She covered her mouth to withhold a throaty sob, hastily wiping her tears away before doling out the gruel into the only remaining unsmashed bowls they owned.

Every day since that Christmas day her mother died, it had seemed like the continuation of some terrible nightmare. The horrifying visions never seemed to end no matter how many times she closed her eyes or came awake. The pain in her heart was like a knife being twisted, her legs wobbled to the point she had to grab the back of a nearby chair for support.

The sound of her father's heavy footsteps snapped her out of her reverie, Meg set the table and poured her father's coffee just as he rounded the corner. His stubble was unkempt and disheveled, his eyes bloodshot from the hangover that was making his steps unsteady. His bald head was gleaming with sweat, the nightclothes he was dressed in straining to contain his belly.

He winced as a beam of sunlight managed to fall across his face for a moment as he passed through the small room that divided the kitchen from the bedroom, his hand moved up to shield himself. The thin, ugly smile that tugged at his lips was a shadow of the full, loving one that Margaret had known as a child.

"I see you made breakfast on time for once," he said dismissively, his eyes glittering dangerously as he settled down into his chair. He raised the cup of coffee to his lips, ensuring that the sound of his sipping echoed across the room. "I wish you would learn not to leave the coffee on the fire so long."

"I'm sorry, Papa. I tried not to leave it on as long this time," she replied pleasantly, doing her best to be pleasing to him. He could berate her all he wanted. So long as he wasn't violent, she could deal with anything he had to say. "I can try and get you some more today."

She was raising her spoon to her lips when the solid thud of a fist pounding on their front door shattered the silence of their breakfast. Margaret's green eyes widened as her spoon clattered back into her bowl. What was it? She glanced back at her father questioningly.

The expression on his face was both grave and vicious, silencing the questions that had been forming on her tongue.

The bottle he had been drinking from was held tightly in his hand like a weapon. That told Margaret all she needed to know about the situation. Trouble was coming. He motioned for her to move away from the door, slowly rising from his chair. "Who's there?" he hollered, irritation evident in his voice.

"Joseph Wilshire, this is Constable Jones. I have here with me a Phillip Duncan, who claims that you are three months behind on your rent payments. You can either turn over the money that you owe, or you will be coming with me," came an equally annoyed voice from the other side. A particularly vicious slam against the door caused a fist-sized hole to appear as a gloved hand punctured through the thin wood.

"If you want me, you are going to have to break that door down," Joseph said, hurtling his bottle toward the hole in the door and smirking as the hand withdrew.

Margaret winced at the audible curse from the Constable behind the door.

"And don't think I'll come without a fight. You better have brought all of Scotland Yard with you."

Margaret scuttled out of the way as their door was suddenly sent sailing across the kitchen with a sickening bang, knocking the cooking pot to the floor as two uniformed officers stepped through the doorway. The first was Constable Jones, a glimmer of triumph glinting in his dark, brown eyes. His once black hair was now tinged with grey, clashing slightly with the blue uniform that he wore. His helmet was noticeably absent, something that struck her as odd.

"Afraid that I couldn't quite invite everyone to come along, but I did bring Inspector Thompson here. He has a special knack for bringing in unwilling prisoners," Jones replied, his gaze lingering for a moment on Margaret before focusing on Joseph.

Thompson was smiling, but there was nothing remotely friendly in the look on the scrappy young officer's face. He flexed his fingers in anticipation, sizing up Joseph with a challenging look. Constable Jones cleared his throat gently, the snap of his fingers dampened slightly by the gloves of his uniform. "Seize him."

Joseph tried to launch himself over the table at Inspector Thompson, but the officer was prepared for that possibility. His hand closed into a fist as his arm drew back, firing a punch into Joseph's face as he was in mid-air. Joseph dropped heavily to the floor, shattering the kitchen table and sending their breakfast scattering across the floor. Thompson moved forward and handcuffed Joseph's hands behind his back as the drunkard groaned on the floor, his eyes moving toward Margaret. "Are you his daughter?"

"Yes," Margaret replied quietly, still quite shaken from how violent the officers had been.

"If you have no other family or guardians, you will be required to be sent to the workhouse until you become of age. How old are you?" Constable Jones had stepped past Inspector Thompson, the older man seeming to radiate a fearsomely smug aura. "You couldn't be much older than fifteen, am I right?"

"She's eighteen," Joseph's voice came across groggily from where Inspector Thompson had propped him up against the wall. His head was bobbing back and forth slowly, obviously concussed by the punch Thompson had struck him with.

"She just came to stay for a bit before she heads off to her future."

"A shame she has to see you in this condition," came a third voice, a weasley man in a pressed brown suit stepping through the door. "I hope that she is more morally responsible than her father has ended up being."

"Mr Duncan."

Margaret struggled to hide her look of disgust as he strode into their home. His brown eyes glittered as he looked over at Margaret. His slicked back hair was greasy, though whether from pomade or filth she couldn't tell.

"Unless you can pay off his debts, I'm dreadfully afraid all of this is now mine."

Margaret swallowed her anger. "Take it. I am not responsible for his debts, so work out your grievance amongst the two of you. I will just require a few days, and then I will vacate the premises."

"Truly, I am dearly sorry," he smirked, chuckling evilly as he started making his way toward the hallway.

Inspector Thompson had long since disappeared with her father down the stairs, leaving Margaret alone with Constable Jones and the greasy debt collector. The

Constable gave Mr Duncan a disapproving look, which Mr Duncan returned with a scowl.

"Well she's clearly already marked for hardship, Constable. Just look at her face." Mr Duncan almost spat.

Margaret raised a hand to her birthmark. The skin there felt like it was burning now from the embarrassment. She pushed her hair in front of her face to try and cover it.

With one final sneer, Mr Duncan turned and was gone.

Margaret let out a sigh of relief only when the sound of his footsteps had completely faded.

Constable Jones crossed his arms in front of his chest. He looked over at Margaret, seeming to notice her youthful appearance for the first time. "You had best watch yourself around him. Mr Duncan will be returning shortly with some movers and a clerk. Once they repossess the furniture in here, they will do nothing further with this place until you have vacated the premises. There will be nothing to prevent anyone from getting in here, so I would recommend figuring out a way to blockade your door before you sleep every night."

Something about the way he said that made her shiver, her arms moved of their own accord to wrap around herself. The hopelessness of her situation was slowly starting to dawn on her, but she couldn't let Constable Jones know that. The workhouse was something she could not face. Life had been hard but that was far worse.

She nodded at him vaguely, watching as he slowly made his way toward the wide doorway, stepping over the broken bits of the splintered door as he went.

"Remember that you said you would only take a few days to be gone. He is going to hold you tightly to that. I wish you luck, Miss Wilshire. May you find good fortune in the coming days." He bobbed his head in a customary bow before vanishing, leaving Margaret alone with the destruction.

Heaving a heavy sigh, she stood and tossed the food into the nearby rubbish bin along with the remnants of the broken dishes. Wiping her hands clean on a nearby towel, she went to the bedroom and changed into a draped skirt. It was one of the nicer outfits that she possessed thanks to the generosity of a neighbourhood seamstress. It would help her look presentable enough that she could try and find work of some kind. At worst, perhaps someone would see her walking around and offer her lodging. Anything would be better than remaining in the house that would soon be stripped bare of anything of worth.

She placed her few nice dresses and the few remaining pieces of her mother's jewellery into a makeshift knapsack she had made from her thin woolen blanket, tossing it lightly over her shoulder before making her way out to the street.

She didn't know where she was going to go, or what she was going to do. As she began to take the first few steps away from what had been the only home she has ever known, tears streamed down her face. She was on her own, for now, and while she was free from her father's constant abuse, she couldn't muster up even the smallest smile. How would she cope? How would she live?

CHAPTER 2

The September air that blew past her as Margaret made her way down to the curb. Nichol Road was as icy as the chill that had settled in the pit of her stomach. She was hungry; the faint gurgling sounds and the ache that gnawed at her mind reminding her painfully of her interrupted meal. It may not have been much, but a bowl of gruel was a far sight better than starving. *Maybe Sally will take pity on me and sell me a piece of bread for cheap.*

Sally was the daughter of Edmond Saliere; A young woman with as much kindness as her father before her. They had become friends thanks to their mothers, but Margaret had seen very little of Sally in the aftermath of Margaret's mother dying. It was easy to recognize her bubbly demeanor as Margaret approached the front of the bakery. The baker's daughter was holding a tray of freshly baked bread. "Fresh bread, Peck loaf's, Quartern's all fresh!"

"How much can two pennies get me?" Margaret stepped forward, plucking the last two coins she possessed and holding them out to her. "I'll take but a small piece if that is all you may give me. I wouldn't want to anger your father."

Sally looked at Margaret for a long moment, her eyes filled with blatant dissociation. As if she was doing everything in her power to act like they had never known one another. "I can give a quartern, but only because my good Christian nature compels me to do so. I am afraid that is the most kindness I may give you, since seeing a fellow woman in obvious distress does my heart ill. But know that this is a kindness I shall grant this time alone. My father will be very displeased when he finds me short at the end of the day."

"I'm ever so grateful. Thank you; I'll not darken the front of your shop any longer," Margaret said, taking the large loaf of bread that Sally handed her and cradling it in her hands. She nodded once more to Sally and made her exit, walking past the other shops as she made her way along the street. She ripped off a piece and bit into the bread, nibbling at it sparingly. Who knew when she would be able to eat again.

Margaret spent the rest of the day walking to the different shops within ten streets surrounding her home, inquiring at each one about possible work. She was turned away by the snooty owner of the nearby seamstress shop. The older woman taking one look at the tatty and faded outfit that Margaret wore and wrinkling her nose in disgust. She had gestured silently at her door dismissively, then turned her back on Margaret.

The chimney sweeps wanted young boys who would work for little wages, and the sailors simply weren't her kind of crowd. She got her fill of their jeering when she walked past the harbour on most days. Even now the memory caused her to pull her petticoat closer against a sudden chill not caused by wind.

It was a twenty-minute trek for Margaret to return home, pausing at the bottom of the front steps of her building to adjust her shoe. Upending it, she was surprised to discover that a small pebble had managed to slip inside. When she entered, she was not surprised to find the place had been stripped of anything that might have been remotely useful. Biting back her tears, as she pulled open the cupboards to find even their kettle had been taken. *Not like there was anything here for me to cook anyway.*

She lit a small candle that had been missed and used it to light her path, noting with gratitude that the movers had chosen to leave behind her uncomfortable pallet. Every other speck of their belongings were gone; her childhood home now a husk of its former glory. *Two days and this place will probably be rented off to the next poor soul who finds themselves trapped here on the Old Nichol Road.*

She set herself upon her cot in the space where her parent's bed had once stood, sighing as she gazed up at the ceiling. She broke off another small piece of bread and ate it, willing her stomach to stop rumbling so much. When thirst overpowered her she made her way toward the back of the building, drawing a bucket of water from the nearby well and taking a deep draught from it. She didn't pay any mind to the small bits of water that flowed down her chest as she drank, intent only on quenching her thirst and alleviating her still gnawing hunger.

Margaret spent the better part of the night tossing and turning fitfully, her dreams filled with faceless men kicking down her door. As the shadowy face of the figure tilted down at her, her stomach rolled as she saw the face of Mr Duncan leering down at her.

She woke with a start and did not return to sleep until the sun had begun to filter in through her window. Her exhaustion finally caused her to return to sleep, nodding off and on until the tolling of the nearby church bell brought her fully awake once again.

Refreshed but hungry, Margaret broke off half of the loaf of bread and had a hasty breakfast. Doing her best to make herself presentable, she made her way into town once more. She went farther than she had the day before, going as far as Worship Street and Hackney Road to seek employment. Most of the shopkeepers simply laughed in her face. The women were far crueler than the men. Most mocked her outfit, asking how she could consider herself presentable in that state. Their words stung, a few of the ruder women causing her to leave their shop in tears. Many times, they would find a way to bring up her birthmark, always in a way to degrade her further.

Two days passed with much of the same, Margaret found herself growing increasingly desperate. The thought of pawning some of her mother's jewellery had come to mind more than once. Shame had so far prevented her from doing so. She felt increasingly weak, every day requiring her to drink more water to try and compensate for her lack of food. She felt bloated when she walked, and had to stop to relieve herself more often than she would have liked in the various dirty alleyways. It was humiliating, but she endured it.

When the day for her to vacate her house came, it was a miserably rainy one. Margaret had done her best to stay under the various awnings of different shops, sheltering from the rain until the shop owners would come out and tell her to get lost. The rain let up around sunset, Margaret did her best to warm up with a fire she had started in one of the nearby rubbish bins. It wasn't a large fire, but large enough to grant her some warmth and help to dry out her clothing. She kept a wary eye on the various other homeless people that she came across, though most of them seemed so caught up in their own problems that they didn't give her a second glance.

When it was finally time for her to lay down, she sighed as she set her thin bedroll on the ground. Since her blanket was being used to keep her clothing out of the elements, she would have nothing to cover up with that night. She spent the night cold and miserable, huddled for warmth beneath a small bridge leading into Bethnal Green, using the nearby bush to help conceal her from any unwelcome eyes. As she lay there, she allowed the first of many bitter tears to flow.

It was when the seventh day had passed and the last of her bread had long since been eaten that Margaret made the decision to go to the docks. Every step she took felt like her feet were weighted down; the accumulated days of walking for miles and sleeping on the hard, cold ground was not doing favours for her.

She had tried everything she could think of for the last week and had walked many streets to no avail, now she felt like she was running out of options. The painful emptiness in her stomach was growing to be more than she could take. As she rounded the corner she bumped into a well-dressed man, gasping as the impact caused her to fall back onto her rear end.

"I'm so sorry; I didn't see you there, sir," she gushed, looking up at the scowling face of the man in front of her. He had a faint scar that ran along the length of his cheek, most likely the reminder of a drunken brawl many years ago. "I was just looking for some work."

"Then you bumped into the right man today, young lady," his blue eyes glinted as he spoke, his tongue sliding along his thin lips. "Where are my manners? They call me Sly; You could say I'm your man if you are in need of work. If you'd like, you and I could work out an agreement. After all, I am sure a lady of your assets could be quite useful. I can make it worth your while; see to it that you are taken care of so long as you work hard."

Margaret's blood ran cold. "No." She was finally able to mutter through her dry mouth.

"I'm sorry, what was that?" Sly flashed a smile of yellow teeth.

"I said," Margaret was finally able to talk more steadily. "I said, no. I won't do what you want me to. Please leave me alone!"

He lunged for her, his hand enclosing around her wrist before he yanked her to her feet. Panic flew through her, her leg lashing out in self-defense. He let out a howl of pain as her leg managed to connect with his shin; his grip loosened on her just enough for Margaret to wrench herself free. She bent down just long enough to grab the corner of her knapsack, not caring as one of her dresses toppled out onto the cobblestones. Simply tucking the loose corner back into place, Margaret ran as fast as her legs could carry her. Sly's curses soon faded in the distance, the only sounds now being the slap of her footwear on the cobblestones and her ragged breathing.

She bit her bottom lip as she did her best to hold back the angry tears that pricked at the corners of her eyes. It was all her father's fault; If he could have acted like a true man and kept his affairs in order, she wouldn't be skulking the streets like a lost urchin trying to find her next meal. Her stomach rumbled softly, dropping to the ground, she curled into a ball and wept miserably.

Feeling utterly defeated, Margaret finally made a choice, to head to the constable station. She had held off for another five days after the Sly incident, doing her best to keep herself as far from the dock area as she could. Keeping to the shadows most of the time, traveling with her head down, with her long hair covering her birthmark, trying not to be recognized. She had been driven to stealing the occasional apple from the fruit vendors she would pass in the streets. She had almost gotten caught a few times, but the constant traffic in that area of town made it easy to slip into a crowd. The fruit was only a temporary cure, doing little to fill the seemingly bottomless hole that her stomach felt like it had become.

She was relieved to see no trace of either Constable Jones or Inspector Thompson upon her arrival; that would serve to alleviate the anxiety she felt. *I will just ask to speak to my father. The worst that they can tell me is that I can't see him. Not like I'll be any worse off either way; I doubt he will have any good advice for me.*

She stopped in front of the clerk's desk, her gaze falling on the disinterested looking young man who couldn't have been older than twenty sitting before her. He was dressed in a blue uniform that she had come to expect from people in his profession, his helmet perched on top of what was probably a fine mess of hair beneath. His blue eyes followed her as she approached, clearing his throat gently before asking, "Can I help you, Ma'am?"

"I am looking for Joseph Wilshire. Your officers came to apprehend him a short while ago, and I was merely wondering if it would be possible for me to visit with him for a little while." Margaret tried not to sound as desperate as she felt. "I promise that it won't take more than a few moments."

"Are you his daughter? Constable Jones did mention that you might drop by at some point. I am afraid that I will be unable to fulfill your request." His eyes watched the look of surprise that crossed her face.

"May I ask why not," Margaret did her best to keep her temper, putting on a smile that she hoped would be convincing. "He hasn't gotten himself thrown in lockdown, has he?"

"No, Ma'am, nothing like that. I am afraid that when we brought Joseph in, he was displaying signs of illness. He became feverish and incoherent, and I am sad to say that he passed earlier this afternoon… despite our best efforts. I am truly sorry for your loss," he said, doing his best to sound sincere. "Is there anything else I can do for you?"

That was it; that was the final nail in her coffin. Her mother's death had come as an unexpected tragedy, and now her father too was no more. She could have cried had it not been for the numbness that was spreading through her. He may have been abusive and neglectful, but he had still been her father. Like it or not, he had put a roof over her head and food in her stomach. He'd been the one constant in her life, and now even that had been taken from her. She was truly alone in the world now. "No, thank you. You've done quite enough," Margaret finally managed to say, turning to leave.

"Oh, Miss, before you go," he exclaimed, rising from his desk so abruptly that she froze in fear. "Constable Jones has a message for you. He says that if you seek to find good employment, make your way over to Barnes. It is a well-to-do neighbourhood filled with the wealthy. Many are often looking for serving girls or maids, and there is even a boarding school for girls with which you might possibly find employment. He says there should be no problem for a young lady such as yourself to find good, honest work."

The way he said that last bit caused her to swallow, wondering just how much the police knew about her actions over the past twelve days. Had Constable Jones been watching her? Did he know her shame?

"Thank you, I will take his advice." *However, I'll need to find a way to get to Barnes. That was almost ten miles from here.* She sighed as she hefted her knapsack up onto her back once more. *I might as well get started. I won't get there any faster if I keep waiting to leave.*

CHAPTER 3

The words of the officer were still echoing in her mind as Margaret walked, her mind racing. She was starting to run out of ideas as to what she could do, and the gnawing emptiness in her stomach was growing more painful by the day. She didn't know if she would be able to take much more without getting some kind of sustenance inside of her. The weakness would surely make her fall and she doubted if she would be able to get up again.

She would have thanked the Lord for even a bowl of gruel at this point. Her stomach rumbled loudly as she walked, no longer entirely sure what part of London she was in anymore.

As she continued on her way, Margaret began to notice that the houses around her were starting to look a lot nicer than the ones in her old neighborhood. Houses of brick and mortar started to replace the wooden shanties that she was used to, and the number of shops and merchant stalls seemed to triple before her very eyes. Horse-drawn carts and carriages trundled past constantly on the cobblestone roads that lead toward Central London. She found herself having to dodge out of the way many times, the voices of the coachmen cracking like whips in her ears.

The sound of their curses were soon replaced with laughter. The voices of many young women at play filled the air. Margaret felt a pang of jealousy as she rounded the corner, wondering what could be causing them all such mirth.

She stepped up to a huge black gate and wrapped her hand lightly around the thick bar. Gazing past it she could see a gaggle of young women who stood in front of a sizable school building.

"Madame Boynton's School for Girls," she read aloud quietly to herself. Her eyes scanning over the modest wooden sign, posted a few feet past the gate's entrance. *What must it be like to be a student here; I bet none of them worry about anything other than their marks.*

Closing her eyes, Margaret allowed herself to imagine it. She saw herself in a clean skirt and blouse, her hair curled and shining in the sunlight after being freshly washed. She saw herself laughing as she danced in a circle with a bunch of other girls her age. Then singing songs carelessly to the wind. She saw herself taking turns with the others to brush one another's hair and gossip about the young gentlemen that their father's had betrothed them to. She could see herself lying under a tall tree, reading a book while the other girls laughed and chased one another around the schoolyard or held little picnics nearby.

The girls were each dressed in a similar uniform consisting of a blue knee-length dress, white socks leading down to their polished shoes. Their hair gleamed with cleanliness no matter what the shade, the vibrancy of their hair no doubt the work of fancy soaps their parents bought for them. They were the exact opposite of the cold, dirty girl who now stood outside their gate. She even caught sight of a few of them looking in her direction, pointing and hiding their snickering behind their hands. She lowered her head and continued walking onward, doing her best to conceal herself behind the wall that surrounded the schoolyard. She was about to move on when she heard a ruckus coming from the direction of the back of the school. She walked hurriedly in that direction, stopping just in time to prevent herself from walking into the angry-looking old woman who was currently in the act of storming out of the back yard.

"Enough of you and those prissy little know-it-alls," the older woman said in a distinct Cockney accent, her blue eyes blazing. She was dressed in the typical garments of a scullery maid, the outfit looking rather out of place on the older woman. "I will not spend one more moment in this school so long as I am going to continue to be treated so poorly. If I am truly so incompetent, then it will be easy for you to replace me. Good day to you! I only pity whatever poor fool comes along and gets roped into taking my place."

"Oh, come now Wanda, you can't leave now! You are blowing this entire thing out of proportion," cried out an exasperated voice. A woman looking to be in her mid-forties was striding purposefully after the old woman. She wore wide-rimmed spectacles over her brown eyes, her hair was pulled back in a tight bun to keep it out of her face. The woman was not overweight, but her stomach and rear did have a pronounced roundness to them. "I'm sorry if what I said offended you. It's just that we've had some complaints lately about a lack of seasoning on the meat. I need to start preparing the meals for the girls, and dinner is only a couple of hours from now. How am I supposed to prepare enough food for them all by myself?"

"I don't care, Abigail!" Wanda replied petulantly, her arms crossed in front of her chest in obvious annoyance. "Maybe you should have thought about that before you insulted my cooking. I have been cooking longer than you've been alive, yet you have the audacity to tell me that I am not following the correct recipe for lamb shank? I was cooking lamb long before you were a twinkle in your father's eye."

"Wanda, please, we can talk about this inside. You are going to cause a scene and make the girls come back and investigate. Or worse, the headmistress herself might come down," Abigail replied, her hands grasped together in a pleading manner. "You can quit when dinner is over, okay? Please don't abandon me, at the last moment, with no help."

"I'm sorry, Abigail. I cannot put up with the disrespect here for a moment longer. I wish you luck in your endeavors, and tell Madame Boynton that she can send the last of my pay to my home address." Wanda stomped off without another word, leaving Abigail standing there looking hopeless.

"I can't believe she would do this to me," Abigail whispered, her hand moving up to scratch nervously at her cheek. "What am I supposed to do now? Who could I possibly find who would be able to help me on such short notice? Madame Boynton will fire me if I don't prepare the meals on time."

"Maybe I could help," Margaret offered quietly. "I may not know how to make everything, but I am a quick learner, and I know that you could use a spare pair of hands in the kitchen. I used to cook for my father, so I'm not entirely without knowledge."

Abigail slowly turned to look at her, blinking as she finally seemed to notice the grubby-looking girl before her. She looked in the direction of Wanda's retreating back, then back to Margaret. Margaret could hear the disappointment in the woman's audible sigh, as she slowly turned and began to walk away.

Margaret felt tears prickle at the corner of her eyes when it seemed like her offer of help was being refused.

The woman had only taken a couple of steps when she began to speak. "Didn't you say you wanted to help? Come along then."

"I'm sorry, Ma'am. Your silence made me think that you were refusing my offer," Margaret said apologetically, quickly following. "Does that mean you will take me on as the new maid?"

"I guess having you is better than trying to do everything myself," Abigail muttered, her hand pressing against Margaret's back as she began to guide her toward the kitchen. "But I can't have you touching any of the food while you are as filthy as you are. Wash yourself in the washbasin and I'll fetch you a uniform. Try to be quick about it; we have a lot of work to do."

Margaret wasted very little time in making herself clean enough that she felt presentable. After almost two weeks of sleeping outside and being unable to bathe, it was nice to feel the layers of dust and grime wiped away from her skin. The outfit that Abigail gave her fit her surprisingly well despite the mature woman not having Margaret's measurements, though it was a little loose as she had lost so much weight.

She took a moment to look at herself in the reflection of a nearby serving tray, admiring just how different she looked compared to the lost little orphan who had entered only twenty minutes ago. She giggled gently to herself as she curtsied to her reflection, turning in time to find Abigail watching her. "Are you finally done in here? We have work to do."

"Yes, Ma'am," Margaret replied eagerly, following after the older woman as she led the new scullery maid back to the kitchen. "I am ready to do whatever you need me to."

"I am glad you sound so eager; it's good to have someone whose spirits haven't been crushed yet," Abigail said, motioning toward a wooden chair that sat in front of a table upon which rested a sizable basket filled with potatoes. "You can start by peeling those potatoes, and try not to lop off any fingers while you do it. You won't be any good to me if you start lopping off body parts."

"I'm sorry, but I haven't ever peeled a potato before," Margaret closed her eyes and braced herself for the hit that she expected, but no hit came. When she opened her eyes again, Abigail was gazing up at the ceiling with a look of exasperation. Not wanting to enrage her, Margaret picked up a potato and a knife and began trying to peel it. She pressed the blade against the potato and slowly began to turn it, peeling it the way her mother used to peel her apples. The long string of potato skin spiraled downward until it finally broke, dropping into the rubbish bin that Abigail had placed beneath her.

"You aren't too bad at that," Abigail said softly, the first small smile that Margaret had seen from the woman appeared on her face. "Maybe this won't be a complete disaster after all."

The two women laboured together for the next few hours, the old clock in the corner of the room chiming with the passing of each hour. Margaret had managed to make short work of the potato peeling, the fruits of her labour were now bubbling in a large pot in the hearth. They had moved on to meat preparation, the scent of the searing meat as it cooked over a spit caused Margaret's stomach to rumble loudly. "Abigail, can I please have something to eat?"

"We don't have time for that right now. You can eat once we make sure that all the students are fed on time," Abigail retorted, her eyes glittering dangerously as she looked over at Margaret. "And you better not try and sneak anything when you think I'm not looking. The Headmistress is very strict when it comes to such things, and I have no doubt that she would punish you greatly should she see you stealing. The last maid who was caught doing so was shamed by the Headmistress in front of the whole school before being fired on the spot."

Margaret swallowed bitterly, closing her eyes as she fought back a wave of nausea. She covered her mouth, her other hand moving to press against her stomach gently. She bit back the angry retort that had risen to her tongue, glowering as she turned her attention instead to kneading bread dough. She had already waited how many days to be able to eat; why should she have to wait until after a bunch of pampered schoolgirls got to eat? She doubted any of them had gone even a single day without food, let alone almost two weeks that she had already gone without anything. She wiped her eyes with the back of her sleeves, not wanting her feelings to show to the rather callous head cook.

"Finally done," Abigail exhaled with relief as she slid down onto a nearby stool, resting her back against the lengthy wooden prep table that took up a quarter of the kitchen. She glanced over at the clock, her eyes widening slightly. "And not a moment too soon. I will go get the cart so we can move everything over to the dining hall. Remember what I said about stealing, Little Mouse."

Then she was gone, leaving Margaret alone in the kitchen. The mouthwatering smell of freshly baked bread and beef stew with potatoes filled her nose, her stomach rumbling far louder this time. *I worked my hands to the bone to help prepare this food. It is only right that I should be able to have some to reward myself. I'll just take a small piece of bread. If I eat the whole thing quickly, no one will have to know. They can't possibly begrudge me a single piece.*

Licking suddenly dry lips, Margaret slowly stepped over to where the loaves of bread were now cooling, eyeing a small piece of bread roughly half the size of her closed fist. She took it gently in her hand and raised it slowly to her lips. After all this time, she was finally going to have something to eat. It would be real food, not the handful of berries or occasional apple she managed to pilfer from one of the less observant merchants when they weren't looking.

She lifted the slice of bread to her mouth and took a ravenous bite, chewing as quickly as she could. Every second that she took was another second closer to Abigail returning and catching her in the act, and that was the last thing Margaret wanted. After almost two weeks of practically nothing in her belly, the taste of the bread was enough to cause tears to flow down her face. She took one bite after another, not caring about how undignified she might look while doing so. She was so caught up in what she was doing that she barely registered the soft tapping of shoes and a cane, on the stairway, her eyes moving toward the door as a shadow fell across the doorway.

"Now, what do we have here? Would you care to tell me why you are standing in my kitchen and eating food meant for my students? Where is that cook, Abigail?" the older woman's questions were like a barrage, each question like a glancing blow to Margaret. "Do you know what I do to people who come into my kitchen thinking they can just help themselves?"

Margaret felt her throat constrict slightly, swallowing roughly as she looked at the woman. Judging from the way she carried herself, she had to be quite an important person. She was dressed in a rather expensive-looking blue dress over a number of petticoats, a cane with a handle carved in the shape of a wolf held tightly in her bony right hand.

After taking a moment to settle her nerves, Margaret took a deep breath before speaking.

"I wasn't just helping myself, Ma'am. I just helped Abigail finish preparing all of the food and found that I couldn't resist. I know that Abigail told me to wait, but I just couldn't. It was just to tide me over; I didn't mean any harm by it. I even took the smallest piece of bread there was so that I wouldn't be depriving any of the students of the good stuff," Margaret said, her head hanging with the piece of bread still held in her grasp. "I wouldn't have done it, but I haven't eaten in days and feared I might faint if I didn't eat something soon."

"Is that so?" The woman replied softly, her eyes glittering as she spoke. "Well, I am sure that Abigail will be most displeased to hear that you disobeyed her direct order. What good is a maid who cannot follow simple instructions?"

Margaret's cheeks burned with humiliation, trying her best to keep her temper in check. What right did this woman have to shame her for wanting to eat? If this old woman had found herself without food for almost two weeks, she would be clawing at the walls for anything to put in her stomach too. *Why is it that every time I try to do anything that I am constantly shamed for it? I am just trying to survive! I didn't realize that the world was so full of cruel, uncaring people.*

"Would you care to tell me where Wanda went? That old bat is supposed to be helping Abigail prepare everything," the woman said, finally taking the topic of conversation from Margaret's supposed crime to something else. "Don't tell me that she and Abigail got into another fight and she stormed off? I told those two that if they couldn't communicate to one another with politeness and decorum not to bother speaking."

"From what I overheard as I was walking past, the argument started over Abigail telling Wanda that she wasn't seasoning the lamb shanks correctly," Margaret offered helpfully, hoping that this meant that her infraction was being forgiven for now.

The woman's eyes rolled so hard that Margaret feared they might pop out of her head. "I'm surrounded by fools," she muttered, turning her head at the sound of the wooden meal cart being pushed down the hallway. "Ah, that must be Abigail now."

Abigail emerged around the corner, the cart creaking as it moved. "All right, Little Mouse. Let's get everything loaded onto the cart and wheeled out to the dining room. Once everything has been portioned out, we can come back here and I'll make you a plate to thank you for all your hard work..." Her words trailed off as she suddenly noticed the old woman standing behind Margaret, the cook's face paling. "H-Headmistress, what are you doing down here?"

"One of the girls came and reported to me that they heard loud hollering coming from the back of the school. They were understandably worried since they could hear the commotion all the way from the back to the front yard, so I told them I would come to investigate. And do you know what I found when I arrived? Your little helper helping herself to a piece of bread," the Headmistress replied, her finger tapping on the top of her cane's handle lightly.

Abigail turned to look at Margaret, a pained expression on her face. "Why? I told you that we just had to wait a little longer," she said, the disappointment in her voice was hurting Margaret more than if she had been yelling.

"I'm sorry," Margaret said, tears brimming in the corners of her eyes. "I was just so hungry."

The look of pity on Abigail's face was in stark contrast to the stern, unwavering look of the Headmistress. "Abigail, I want you and our new friend here to go serve dinner. When that is finished, bring her up to my office. I wish to have a word with her in private. We will need to discuss the matter of her theft in more detail and discuss compensation."

"I don't have any money," Margaret protested, looking at Abigail pleadingly to intervene on her behalf. The other woman simply looked away from her, busying herself with starting to load everything onto the cart. Margaret sighed and stepped forward to help, figuring there was nothing to do about her situation at that moment. She simply had to focus on the job she had to do, whatever may come later she would face then. She nodded in acknowledgement of the Headmistress's words before pushing the cart, allowing Abigail to guide her down the hallway in what Margaret assumed was the direction of the dining area.

The hustle and bustle of dinner kept her mind occupied, Abigail was barking out orders to her about how to portion each plate while the students chatted excitedly in line, each awaiting their turn. Margaret's stomach was still rumbling from being so close to such amazing smelling food, but the knowledge that she would soon be chastised by the Headmistress had robbed her of any appetite she might have had. It was nice to have work to distract her from her own situation, but she had the feeling her employment was going to prove to be short-lived. When the last of the students had come up to grab their plate and the dining room was filled with the sound of cutlery on plates, Abigail finally turned to Margaret. "Good work, Little Mouse. I only hope that you manage to stick around after your talk with the Headmistress."

"That makes two of us," Margaret muttered, taking off her apron and hanging it over the back of one of the nearby chairs. "Are you going to take me up there?"

"Yes, we'll be going to see her now," Abigail replied solemnly. "I just hope that she takes it easy on you."

They walked together in silence up a long flight of spiral ascending stairs, the only sound that of their footsteps echoing. Once they reached the landing, Margaret's eyes moved to focus on the solid wooden door that stood at the end of the hall. She shivered as she felt an intense sensation of foreboding, wrapping her arms around herself to ward off the sudden chill she felt. She started walking toward the door, blatantly aware that Abigail had not moved with her.

"What do you like to be called?" Abigail's voice caught Margaret by surprise, her head tilted to the side as she considered for a moment.

"I suppose I don't mind what you call me. I am Margaret, but my father used to call me Meg. I suppose either would be fine."

Good luck, Meg," Abigail called softly. "I'll be waiting here for you."

CHAPTER 4

"I was beginning to wonder if you were going to run off with your tail between your legs rather than come in to see me," Winifred said as soon as Margaret opened the door. The older woman was sitting in a high-backed, expensive wood and leather chair. She had a cigarette lit in one hand, the end glowing bright red like a cherry, as she took a deep inhale before expelling a thick cloud of white smoke.

The room was remarkably well furnished. A glass bottle filled with brandy immediately caught Margaret's eye, the light reflecting off it from the late afternoon sunshine filtering in through the window blinding her momentarily.

As she tried to blink the black spots out of her vision, she tried to look around at the rest of her surroundings. There was a tall bookcase near the back of the room that was practically filled to bursting with tomes. Candles burned atop highly polished brass candlesticks, the smoke coming from them filtering out of the window that had been flung fully open. A silver timepiece glittered from around Winifred's wrist, though Margaret did her best not to let her gaze linger on it. She didn't want to give Winifred more of a bad impression than she already had.

The older woman's eyes watched her steadily as she moved to sit in the only available chair remaining, a short-legged wooden one with no padding to offer relief from the uncomfortable seat. It was the kind of chair one would likely find in the pits of the most insidious dungeon. Margaret found she had to sit up as straight as she could to just barely be able to see above the high wooden desk, amplifying her sensation of being smaller than the woman before her. Winifred still had her cane, her chin resting on top of her hands, which were folded over the handle.

Margeret took a deep breath, praying that her voice remained steady.

"I need this job, Ma'am. Even if I don't get paid much. It would be leagues better than having to continue living on the streets," she said, noting the way that the headmistress's eyes had narrowed while she spoke. "If you offer me somewhere to stay and a meal a day, I will be content. Perhaps a few shillings a week for compensation for hours laboured?" Margaret was using the words her father's old work buddies had used to use when they'd be over for drinks after long hours at the coal mine. She knew she didn't really have much room to bargain, but at the very least, she knew she had shown up at an opportune time. There was no harm in trying to sway the situation somewhat in her favor. "I was such a help to Abigail today; the least you could do is give me a chance."

"It is true that you managed to help divert a rather troublesome situation, but that doesn't erase the fact that you explicitly disobeyed your superior. When Abigail told you not to eat, you should have listened. How can I consider hiring you when my first interaction with you involved berating you over breaking the rules?" Winifred's eyes were glittering as she spoke, her smile revealing the missing teeth in her mouth. The gloating look on her face was that of a predator who had backed its prey into a corner. "What have you to say to that?"

"I am more than willing to work off the bread that I ate if you believe I should. I ask that you excuse my conduct today. I have spent the last two weeks experiencing the worst time of my life. I have slept in the cold and damp, have gone days at a time without food, and have managed to survive only on water. I had to endure the scents of everything cooking for hours, and my hunger caused me to err in my judgement. I only hope that you can forgive me and allow me to prove myself capable of following orders," Margaret replied, slightly put off by the smile that was tugging at the corner of Winifred's mouth.

"You set an awful lot of demands for a thief," Winifred snapped, her words cracking against Margaret like a whip.

"What would your parents say if they knew what you were doing?"

"I am an orphan, Ma'am. My mother died when I was eight-years-old. I remember how she died. It was because of the coal in the air... She died with me beside her. But... my father would always claim she was one of the many victims of Jack The Ripper. I think it was just a lie he told people to get pity at the pub," she said, rolling her shoulders gently. "I am not a thief; I worked enough for it. I don't see why I have to answer for it at all. It was a portion that would have been doled out to me eventually, yet you insist on treating me as though I stole jewellery or gold."

"What became of this drunken father of yours?" Winifred asked brusquely, ignoring Margaret's previous comment. Her eyes were twinkling strangely now, her gaze seeming to burrow deep into Margaret. "Where is he now? Was he so much of a failure that he couldn't keep his family sheltered? Is he off skulking in some alleyway hoping to drown his problems in cheap whiskey?"

"He took ill when taken to the debtor's prison and passed on a few days ago," Margaret replied, feeling frightened at how steady and calm her voice was while she talked about his death. "He left me with nothing but a few outfits and a blanket and allowed our very home to be taken from us. Rather than wanting to be thrown into the workhouse because of my youthful appearance, I decided to set off on my own to try and find employment. I tried a variety of places and met a variety of people, but none would offer me employment or offered jobs that were acceptable to me."

"The debtor's prison? My my; your entire family sounds to be filled with riff raff and other unsavory sorts. No wonder you would resort to thievery; your whole family is a band of scoundrels," Winifred spat, rising slowly from her chair and pointing a finger accusingly at Margaret. "Do you truly expect me to take in the daughter of a man who couldn't pay his debts on her word alone? Do I look like some foolhardy old crone who will accept your sob story at face value and welcome you in like a family member?"

"I am not like my father," Margaret protested, her words bubbling out of her before she could stop herself. "I am not nearly as immature and short-sighted as he was, nor is my every thought centered around how and when I will have my next drink. I do not incur debts without thought to pay them off, and my word is my bond. If I have promised to do something, then I shall not stop until it is done. That is how my mother was, and that is how I am striving to be."

Winifred looked taken aback that Margaret would dare respond to her in such a manner. Margaret could see the woman's knuckles turning white from how tightly she was gripping her cane, trying and failing to conceal the rage that flashed intermittently across her face.

"What good is your word that you won't steal from me again? You will have to prove yourself if you hope to even think that you will continue to work here after that little stunt. You'll work for the next few days without pay. I shall be merciful and allow you the meal you requested, but it will be the leftover scraps from dinner each day. I'll be sure to inform Abigail not to overfeed you, and if I find that even a small bit of extra food is missing I will fire you on the spot. Or better, I'll call in the police and they can string you up in the gallows just like they do all the other thieves and riff raff."

"Thank you; I will do my utmost to meet your expectations," Margaret replied softly, doing her best to meet the Headmistress's gaze but faltering from the ugly look the woman gave her. She couldn't shake the feeling that there was something nefarious behind Winifred's interest in her. *I'm going to have to make sure I keep an eye on this woman. She doesn't exactly strike me as having my best interests in mind.*

"There are just a few simple rules you will need to follow. For one, don't eat outside of the allotted times. You get one meal for each day worked, and you eat after everyone else. That is simply how it is here. You do not make eye contact with the other girls for any reason, and you will address any of them that speak to you the same way you would address me. Unlike you, they are being groomed into being fine young ladies of high society so they can be of some use," Winifred continued, acting as though she hadn't heard what Margaret had just said. "I don't care what insults they hurl at you or what they do, you must remain courteous at all times. Believe me; I will find out if you speak out of line to one of my girls. Word travels to me quickly around here."

"I can do that," Margaret nodded. "What will my official position be?"

"You will be a scullery maid, of course. I have to have someone to replace Wanda now that Abigail has caused her to walk off the job," Winifred snarled, her gnarled finger pointing at Margaret poignantly. "You will be responsible for helping Abigail in the kitchen and doing the cleaning around the place. Abigail will be able to tell you the list of daily chores, and I expect you to have them memorized by the time the week is out. Don't let me catch you setting even a toe out of line, or I will make it so you would never show that scarred face of yours in London ever again."

The tone of her voice left no doubt that she meant every word, and Margaret repressed a shudder as she nodded. Her fingers itched to go to the birthmark on her face, but she would not let them move.

Nodding in return, Winifred continued. "In the meantime, you may go down to the kitchen and have your meal. After that, have Abigail take you to the servant's quarters and get you introduced to the rest of the lot. You are going to be working closely with them in the coming days, so try not to make too many enemies."

"I won't," Margaret said, rising from her chair and starting to make for the door. "I'll just take my leave then, Ma'am."

"Not just yet; there is still the matter of your punishment. I can't just let you commit a crime and not have you answer for it. That isn't how the world works," Winifred's tone of smug glee sent new fear coursing through Margaret. She had assumed that her punishment was going to be working without pay for a few days. She hardly believed that she should have to submit to a physical punishment as well.

"I hardly think that would be necessary," Margaret protested, her eyes fixated on Winifred slowly making her way around her desk.

"I want you to put your hands on my desk and don't move until I tell you that you may," Winifred said, her hushed voice evoking the same kind of fear that her father's drunken rage once did.

Margaret knew what would come next; it was what had always followed. She would be beaten, probably with the very cane that Winifred's right hand held in a death grip. Margaret swallowed fearfully, her eyes wide with silent horror. She wanted to flee, but there was nowhere for her to run. If she just let this crazy woman do what she wanted this once, she'd have a new place to stay and something to eat. That would be worth a few smacks.

How strong could a woman the headmistress's age possibly be?

Taking a deep breath, Margaret placed her hands flat on the desk and waited, knowing that the thin uniform would offer little protection.

She could hear the wind whistle each time Winifred brought her cane down on the back of her legs. The pain ripped through her, her hands squeezing into fists on the desk as she struggled not to scream. Winifred struck her so many times that she eventually lost track, her nails digging into her palms until she could feel blood oozing out onto her fingers. The back of her legs stung as though they'd been burned.

"That will do for this time," Winifred said.

Margaret wanted to crumple to the floor but she wouldn't.

"You may go."

The beating had stiffened her limbs. Every nerve in Margarets body screamed as she slowly straightened up. It took all of her willpower not to whimper or cry as she stiffly walked toward the door.

"Let that be a lesson to you," Winifred huffed, plopping herself bodily back down onto her chair. Even though the act had taken much strength from her, the satisfaction on the old woman's face was unmistakable. The way her wide mouth stretched upward in a smug smirk reminded

Margaret of a toad who had just swallowed a particularly juicy fly. Margaret made sure to keep her gaze neutral, subservient even.

"Now get out of here. I am tired of looking at you. If you keep your nose clean and do your part, maybe I'll consider keeping you around. For now, you can be content with your new position as a scullery maid. You'll start immediately, so report to Abigail and see if she has any work for you. I'm sure she wouldn't mind having someone to wash the pots."

"What did she do to you?" Abigail asked as she watched Margaret hobble slowly out of the headmistress's office, every step she took made her wince from the stinging on her back side and legs. "She didn't put the cane to you, did she?"

The silent tears that leaked down Margaret's cheeks was enough of an answer.

Abigail clicked her tongue in sympathy, placing her hand on the young girl's shoulder and leading her slowly down the stairs. Margaret was grateful for the kindness that Abigail was showing; it was nice to see that there was someone within this school who wasn't completely cold-hearted. When they got back to the kitchen, Abigail got some ice from the ice chest and wrapped it in a washcloth before resting it against the back of Margaret's legs.

Margaret closed her eyes as the coolness of the ice soothed her bruised and torn flesh. She hadn't gotten a chance to look, but she could tell that she was going to be turning many interesting shades of purple in the next few days. She could almost feel the wooden cane's impression on the back of her legs and lower buttocks. "That could have gone better," she said with a shaky sigh.

"I knew she was going to cane you, but I didn't think she would go so far with it," Abigail said, moving over to where an extra plate of food had been sitting. She carried it over to Margaret. "Here; I know you disobeyed me earlier, but I now know you had your reasons. Why don't you tell me a bit about yourself. How did you get here? I can tell from how dirty and malnourished you look that you've been on hard times."

"It doesn't matter," Margaret said quickly, shaking her head as if to ward off some terrible memory. "My dad... well he's dead now. I have no one else. I am hoping that the time I have to spend here will be brief at best. I will work to earn my keep, I won't stir the pot, and I'll remember to not let my head be raised too high," she added miserably, wincing as she adjusted the cloth and discovered it to be soaked through with water and blood. She sighed and handed it back to Abigail, slowly forcing her legs to straighten as she climbed unsteadily to her feet. "Can you take me to the servant's quarters?"

"I might as well," Abigail said, the portly woman pushed herself to her feet. "It is getting late, and I'll need to show you where you'll be bunking tonight," she added dismissively.

"You don't sound particularly overjoyed. Am I going to have to share a room with you or something?" Margaret joked, but her smile quickly faded when she saw the look on Abigail's face. "Oh... we will be sharing a room, won't we?"

"I'm afraid that with the number of girls that attend the school, spare bedrooms are a bit of a luxury. We, the serving staff tend to double up in rooms, and the other rooms are taken up by married couples and family members. I used to share my room with one of the old maids, but I do believe I mentioned what became of her earlier," Abigail said, her voice echoing in the hallway they now strode down. Oil lamps hung on the walls helping to illuminate the way.

Without having realized it, the majority of the evening had managed to slip past. The last remaining vestiges of colour leftover from the sunset was beginning to fade into the night sky, leaving behind only a pitch blackness occasionally interrupted by small pinpricks of white. The faint light painted their faces temporarily orange when they passed by one of the ornate windows, Margaret held up her hand to shield herself from the sun as it managed to reflect off the window in a blinding way. She was still rubbing the black spots from her eyes when she felt Abigail stop. It was so abrupt she walked into her.

"Here we are. It isn't much, but it keeps out the winter chill and provides a little relief from the summer heat, and that's really all you can hope for nowadays," Abigail said cheerfully, gesturing toward the bedroom that was to be shared between the two of them.

Margaret was relieved to see a second bed sitting close to the opposite wall; even if it was a straw mattress it would still be an improvement over the cot she had used for the last eight years. She almost forgot about the pain in the back of her legs as she moved over to the bed and flopped down on it, ignoring the stinging sensation as she took a moment to let it sink in. *I have my own bed again.*

"You can set up your things over there, and there is that small end table at the foot of the bed where you can keep your possessions. Make sure you don't leave anything you wouldn't want to go missing lying around, as things have a habit of disappearing every now and then," Abigail said, her eyes gazing meaningfully toward the far wall. It looked for a moment like she was trying to peer through it to the other side, the intensity in her gaze was slightly off-putting.

Margaret nodded uneasily, setting her knapsack next to the bed and gently laying her clothing out. She placed a single dress inside the drawer and placed her mother's jewellery beneath it, stacking her other dresses on top of it when she was done. It wasn't much, but she hoped it would be enough to prevent anyone from trying to rummage around when she wasn't there. Perhaps she could look into securing a bit of rope or something with which to seal the drawer when she was away. It wasn't that she distrusted Abigail; but with the warning she had been given it sounded like there was someone here who couldn't be trusted.

"It would be best for you to get some rest now, Margaret. We tend to get an early start. Starting tomorrow, you are going to be responsible for a lot of things that I am certain you have not dealt with before. I will be throwing a lot of things at you in a small amount of time, so do your best to keep up. If you do your best and try not to anger the Headmistress too much, perhaps she will eventually lighten up on you."

"I can only hope so." Margaret replied with a weak chuckle, slowly stretching out onto the mattress and letting out a soft groan as her back popped in multiple places. There was a clean blanket which was such a luxury. It had been so long since she had felt something so soft that the accumulated weariness of the last few weeks seemed to hit her all at once. She was vaguely aware that Abigail was still talking to her, but her voice seemed quiet, like it was coming from far away. Her eyes grew heavy and before she knew it, Margaret was fast asleep. She didn't stir once throughout the entirety of the night, and her usual nightmares were thankfully absent.

CHAPTER 5

Aside from the insistent stinging in her legs that lasted for the first few days, Margaret was in relatively good spirits. The time she spent at the school hadn't been easy by any means, but it was a far cry better than being on the street. Even the scraps that she was given for dinner tasted good because they were warm and filling. With the worries about where she was to rest her head now lifted from her shoulders, she put all her effort into proving herself as a maid. If she wasn't waking up early to start preparing breakfast, she was doing extra cleaning in the corridors. Without complaint she tackled the endless pile of dishes that always seemed to fill up the kitchen, leaving them sparkling clean and her hands stiff and wrinkled.

Despite the less than pleasant vibes she had gotten from the students from passing glances, Margaret found herself being disillusioned very quickly. While she had hoped that their education would be teaching them to treat the servants with a semblance of grace, she quickly discovered that one of their preferred pastimes was harrassing the maids.

It all started one afternoon when she was going through the girl's dormitory to change the bedding. She was accompanied by Annie, a fellow serving girl who was tasked with watching over Margaret in Abigail's absence. Having discovered that Abigail was not the one in charge of the maids and servants, Margaret discovered very quickly that she wasn't going to see Abigail very often. That made her sad, since Abigail had seemed like one of the few servants who was mildly approachable. The rest all gave her the impression that they felt they were better than her, and she got the distinct impression that they were going out of their way to avoid her at times.

She had just finished changing the last of the bedding when she felt like she was being watched. When she turned around, she found she was looking at a green-eyed blonde girl who couldn't have been much older than she was. Judging by the uniform that she was wearing, she was one of the female students. *Probably back early from one of her classes.*

"I'm sorry to intrude, Miss; I'm just changing the bedding. I will get out of your way quickly," she said, gathering the dirty bedding and moving to step past her. She swallowed when the blonde held her hand up in front of her, stopping her in her tracks.

"I saw you outside the gate almost a week ago. Do you care to tell me why you are suddenly working in my school?" the blonde asked, her head shaking slowly from side to side in disapproval. "Headmistress Winifred must be desperate for help if she would stoop to employing someone as lowly as you. Though, I will say you aren't nearly as insufferable as Wanda was. Though, tell me true. Did you really steal food from the kitchen your first day here?"

Margaret kept her gaze averted from the student as her cheeks flushed in embarrassment. "I'm sorry but I really can't stay. I'm not supposed to speak to you." She moved to step around the girl, but the blonde stepped in her way once more.

"Is it true you are a theif?"

"I don't know how you heard about that, but I already made good on my debt," Margaret said wanting desperately to get out of there.

"Is that what you think? That because you've done a little bit of cleaning and cooked a few meals that you can wipe your name clean? The entire school knows you are a thief who happened to be given a chance to redeem herself by our most gracious headmistress. I don't believe your ruse for one minute, and so I shall keep my eyes closely on you. Don't think that I won't hesitate to tell the headmistress should you step out of line," the blonde said with glee, licking her pale pink lips like a predator sizing up its prey.

"I will keep that in mind, Miss," Margaret replied carefully. "I have no intentions of misbehaving; I merely wish to do my work unimpeded and graciously."

"How could you possibly hope to do that with a face as hideous as yours?"

The impact of those words left Margaret winded, her mouth opening and closing soundlessly.

"Tell me, is that a natural birthmark or were you branded as a theif?"

"As far as I know –" Margaret started to respond softly, her throat suddenly dry.

"I was told by my papa that people with marks like yours were branded by the Devil. He told me that those marks were the way for both God and men to know the devil's chosen and to be able to shun them. Your mark is by far one of the biggest that I've ever seen," she said softly, her eyes glittering coldly as she took a step closer to Margaret. "You have the devil's stain," she whispered, her lips a mere inch from the maid's ear.

"My name is Shirley Abbot, and I am the daughter of a very important merchant. My papa can buy me anything I want, and he sent me to this wonderful boarding school so that I could be raised as a proper lady," she said, her hand moving to slap the sheets out of Margaret's hand. An ugly smile sat on her face as she watched the sheets tumble to the floor. Crossing her arms she looked down on Margaret. "I am one of the most popular girls here, and even Madame Boynton favours me. I can do whatever I want to you and I'd never get in trouble," Shirley added, the gleam in her eye making Margaret shiver in fear.

"I will remember," Margaret promised, kneeling down to collect the sheets that she had dropped.

"See to it that you do," Shirley said, laughing at Margaret before making her way out of the room.

Margaret took a deep breath, closing her eyes as she felt a surge of anger bubbling in her chest. *What a spoiled little girl! I do hope that the others here aren't half as disrespectful as she is. I don't think I can put up with much more of this before my temper breaks.*

When Annie found her again, Margaret did her best to not let on that anything was amiss. She just kept the words of Shirley in mind, silently hoping that the other girls would prove to be less ruthless in their treatment of her. Being ignored and shunned would be much easier.

Her fears had proven justified after another week, noticing immediately that many of the other girls seemed to be joining Shirley in making fun of her. She had heard their hurtful words in the hallways as they passed her, or heard whispers from the girls when they thought she wasn't about. She had heard them talk about the birthmark on her cheek, calling her a witch and saying she was branded by the devil. They had mocked her uniform, saying that it looked out of place on a commoner like her. Many of them had taken to calling her Cleaning Witch, the name usually being said in the most disgusted tone they could muster. It wouldn't have hurt so much if she had a friend to confide in, but she was by herself here. Even Abigail proved to be less than sympathetic to her plight.

"Girls are just like that. There's no use letting them get under your skin. All they have are words, and words themselves are harmless. You just need to take pride in who you are and the work that you do. None of them are going to make sure that you get your job done or that you continue to succeed here. You have to do that for yourself. If they get too overwhelming, just distance yourself from them until you've had a moment to calm down. That was one thing Wanda could never figure out how to do, and you saw how she ended up," Abigail said one night over dinner, as the two of them ate together in the kitchen.

"You make it sound so much easier than it is," Margaret protested, her mouth half filled with beef stew. "You should hear the way they talk about me... the way they talk *to* me. I've never heard a more disrespectful group of young ladies in all of my life."

"The fact that they are all from the upper crust probably doesn't help things," Abigail agreed, dunking a small piece of bread in her stew before chewing on it thoughtfully. "They don't know what it feels like to have to claw their way through life. Their parents hand them everything they could ever want on a silver platter."

Margaret gazed out of the nearby kitchen window, enjoying the sight of the full moon as it shone through the glass. *What would that be like,* she wondered? *To never have to worry about where I would rest my head each night. To learn and not have to work myself to the bone just to be able to scrape a living. Could I ever truly be lucky enough to get that? Or is this mark on my cheek truly one of misfortune?*

"Hello there, Cleaning Witch. Did you sell your soul for a bar of soap?" The question came from a chubby brown-haired girl with a wide, dopey-looking face. It was a couple of days later and Margaret was cleaning one of the fireplaces when a group of students had gathered seemingly out of nowhere around her. She hadn't noticed them at first, thanks to the concentration she was putting toward her task, but the instant she was called out to, she became aware of just how many girls were gathered around her.

"Careful, Monica. She might cast a spell on you and cause you to become as poor as she is. You wouldn't want to spend the rest of your life washing dishes and scrubbing floors, would you?" Shirley called out from where she leaned against the nearby wall, watching Margaret with a smug smirk tugging at the corners of her mouth.

Margaret bit her bottom lip and forced herself to keep her gaze on the floor in front of her, positioning her dustpan before sweeping the ashes out of the fireplace. She did her best to ignore them, wiping her forehead when she managed to sweep the rest of the ashes into her dustpan.

"What's the matter, Cleaning Witch? Do you not hear us talking to you?" Shirley called out, moving up beside her and kicking her dustpan, sending the ashes scattering all over the floor.

Shirley and her cronies laughed, the sound echoing in Margaret's ears as her face burned with rage. She realized that she was gripping the hem of her apron extra tightly to prevent them from balling into fists. She reminded herself to calm down; she couldn't do anything to Shirley. The girl was supposedly one of Winifred's favorites, so complaining about her would do no good either.

"That is quite enough of that. For the daughters of the upper class, you are all acting no better than lowly gangsters," came a voice from beside her, the feeling of a hand gently resting on her back caused Margaret to glance upward.

Standing over her was a girl with fiery red hair and fierce blue eyes that glittered with warmth. "I am sure that you and your goons were raised better than that, Shirley."

"What did you just say to me, Braddock?" Shirley's voice came in a soft whisper, her fists clenching at her side as she regarded the redhead coldly.

"You heard me; I am not the kind of person who likes to repeat myself," the redhead replied. Her own eyes burning with defiance as she returned Shirley's glare undaunted. As she stood over her, Margaret, could almost feel a suit of armor held over her body. The girl was like one of the Valkyries from the stories her mother used to read her.

"The maid has enough work to be done without you adding to it. She just cleaned this floor, yet you've gone and made a mess of it again."

"The maid is here because she is working off a debt. Who cares if I make her work a little harder to make up for it. If she didn't want this kind of treatment, she shouldn't have been born a commoner," Shirley shot back, flipping her hair dismissively. "I also don't recall answering to you, Ruth. You had better remember your place as well. In my eyes, you are hardly better than this maid."

"You are the one who should remember her place," Ruth replied, stepping forward and pressing her pointed finger into the center of Shirley's chest. "I happen to have a family that is just as successful as your precious father, and our wealth comes from a lot further back than a couple of generations," she stressed, smirking at the offended look that crossed Shirley's face.

The redhead turned to the rest of the girls, clearing her throat before continuing. "I expect that none of you will give this maid any more of a hard time from now on. Unless you wish to open up a quarrel with me."

Many of the other girls muttered apologies before dispersing, leaving Shirley looking put out as her forces dwindled before her eyes. The blonde bit her bottom lip in irritation, her teeth slowly grinding against one another. "Don't think that this is over, Ruth. Not by a long shot."

"I consider this matter quite settled, actually," Ruth replied cattily, gesturing dismissively in Shirley's direction. The blonde scoffed and spun on her heel, stomping away without so much as a passing glance.

Ruth exhaled shakily once they were alone, turning her attention once more to Margaret. "Are you all right?"

"Yes, Miss. Thank you, Miss," Margaret replied stiffly, her eyes still lowered to the floor. Despite the fact that Ruth had just come to her rescue, it didn't take away the rules that Winifred had given her. She was not supposed to have eye contact without permission.

"You don't have to speak so formally to me," Ruth replied, her soft laughter making Margaret slowly raise her gaze.

The redhead was smiling widely at her, her hand slightly covering her mouth as she waved her hand at Margaret in amusement. "I have to admit that I've never been good with that kind of stuff. It's probably the reason why my mother insisted I be sent here."

"I'm sorry; Winifred told me I wasn't supposed to make

eye contact with any of you," Margaret replied, not wanting to insult her rescuer.

"I don't see why my new friend wouldn't be allowed to look at me," Ruth replied, sounding genuinely dumbfounded.

Margaret blinked in surprise. "Friend? You want to be my friend?" she asked, her tone filled with disbelief.

"You don't seem to have many friends around here, but I can only assume that is because of the gossip that is floating around the school about you. They make you out to be some terrible person, but I do not think you are. I've noticed you working very hard these last few weeks, and I genuinely believe you to be a good person. I just think you need to look up a little more," Ruth said, her hand reaching down to gently push Margaret's hair aside and stroked along her birthmark.

Margaret pulled away reflexively, her hand moving up to cover her cheek. "I'm sorry, I just am so used to trying to hide this mark. All my life I have been mistreated for it, whether by my father in his drunken rages or by your fellow students here. I haven't known pride in myself or for my family for almost seven whole years now."

"Could you tell me more?" Ruth asked, grabbing the broom and trying to start sweeping ashes toward the dustpan.

Margaret immediately let out an inarticulate cry, grabbing the broom out of Ruth's hands and shaking her head furiously.

"You can't do my sweeping. If Winifred or someone were to see, they would say that I was trying to force my work onto one of the students," Margaret said apologetically, a sheepish smile on her face. "I appreciate you being willing to help, though."

"Well, can I stay and watch you sweep while we chat a little longer?" Ruth enquired eagerly.

"I am not sure what you would want to chat about, but I can't exactly tell you not to. You may do whatever you wish," Margaret replied, the broom making a consistent swishing noise as she swept.

"Well, I'm Ruth Braddock, you could tell me your name. That seems as good of a place to start," Ruth pulled up a small chair that sat nearby and straddled it in a very unladylike manner, pressing her chest against the back of it as her chin rested on the top.

"Margaret Wilshire, but my friends call me Meg," Margaret replied, sweeping the last of the ashes into the pan hefting both it and the brush onto her shoulders. "Forgive me if I don't recognize the significance of your last name, Ruth. I am not very well versed with the members of the upper crust."

"I wouldn't expect you to be," Ruth said dismissively, her eyes twinkling as she pulled a small piece of parchment from her pocket and handed it to Margaret. "I know you don't want to run into Shirley more than necessary, so I'll seek you out each day rather than asking you to come back here to the dorms. If anything, I can meet up with you after dinner and keep you company while you work. I promise I won't be too much of a distraction, and in exchange, you can tell me more about yourself."

"Okay," Margaret replied simply, not having the heart to argue with her newfound friend. "I'll look forward to seeing you, then."

"I'm relieved to hear that. I feared you would think me imposing and decline my invitation," Ruth said, reaching her hand out toward Margaret's. "Can I call you Meg?"

"Sure," Margaret grinned despite herself, gathering up her cleaning supplies and looking toward the kitchen. "I should get going. I have some other duties to see to before I can call it a night."

"I won't keep you any longer," Ruth placed her hand gently on Margaret's back, rubbing it gently. "I hope you take care. Rest well tonight."

"You too," Margaret offered a halfhearted wave before scurrying off back to the kitchen. She was greeted by an unhappy Abigail, who chastised her for taking so long on the cleaning. Since Margaret wasn't going to admit that the girls were bullying her, she simply lied and said that she had accidentally knocked over her dustpan.

Abigail had snorted derisively in reply, wiping her hands on the apron currently tied about her waist. "I hope that next time you will act a little more carefully."

"I will, Abigail," Margaret replied, making her way over to where the dinner dishes still sat waiting for her and getting to work. She hummed tunelessly to herself, her spirits soaring the longer she thought about Ruth. She got along relatively well with Abigail, but she was still a subordinate at the end of the day. Abigail was her overseer, and there would always be a polite distance maintained between them because of that professional relationship.

Ruth, however, was different. She had defended Margaret from the other girls and had extended friendship to her. She had spoken endearingly to her, encouraging her not to overlook the simplest of life's joys because she thought she wasn't worthy of them. She had spoken with understanding and not judgement when it came to her birthmark. Even the way that she called Margaret "Meg" felt different than the way everyone else had used it. Only her mother had ever used that name with such kindness in her voice, a thought that brought twin streams of pearly tears dripping steadily down her cheeks.

She didn't mean to cry, but it was almost too good to believe. She half expected to wake up tomorrow to discover that the events of today had all just been a dream, but it was real. When she went to sleep that night, it was a dream of a maiden being rescued by a handsome knight. However, when the knight turned to face her, Margaret found she was instead looking at Ruth's face. There was a radiance around her that seemed to cut through the shadows in her dream, the redhead's voice soothing and gentle.

When she awoke the next day, Margaret's smile just wouldn't go away. As she washed herself with a rag and bucket of cold water, she felt like the joy would cause her heart to burst. *I made a friend. Can you see it, Mama? I made a real friend, and I think she just might be able to help me fix my life.*

CHAPTER 6

The days that passed after meeting Ruth were some of the best Margaret had experienced in a long time. While she still occasionally had to deal with Shirley and some of her friends hurling insults, the majority of the bullying seemed to have been nipped in the bud. True to her word, Ruth had told the other girls to lay off of her, and they were actually listening. No longer did she have to deal with their whispers when she walked by, but she was still wary around them. She always made an excuse to make herself scarce if they tried to hang around her too long.

Ruth managed to meet up with her a lot more than she'd initially assumed would be the case, Margaret even wondering if her new friend was neglecting her studies just to meet up with her. Ruth was an incredibly curious girl and would prod Margaret for information about her past, but she was still hesitant to share that information.

Part of her feared that Ruth would no longer wish to be friends should she discover the truth about her. Another part of her simply didn't want her new friend to pity her. The redhead was one of the few people in the world who had treated her like an equal, and she didn't want to risk doing anything that would ruin that.

They were sitting together on a bench near the front gate one Tuesday night in March, grateful for an excuse to get out of the relatively stuffy school building for a while. Most of the other girls were attending a play that was being hosted in the school's theater, but Ruth had opted to take the time to get to know Margaret better. The redhead had shared with Margaret her own past; she was the daughter of a duke who had been sent to Madame Boynton's because her father didn't think she acted upper-class enough. Apparently she had come to the defense of a servant whom her father had accused of stealing, claiming that another of his guests had taken the object in question and was framing the maid.

"He wasn't willing to trust the word of his daughter enough that he'd be willing to accuse another aristocrat of stealing, so he fired the maid and shipped me off to this school. Little did he know that I am more stubborn than he thinks, and I'm more than capable of playing the part to fool Winifred. However, I'm sure he'll be quite displeased if word of our friendship manages to reach him. He'd say I was doing the very thing I was being punished for in the first place," Ruth said with a laugh, gently fanning herself with the hand fan that she'd brought with her.

"I don't want you to risk punishment for befriending me," Margaret insisted, fidgeting in discomfort from her friend's words.

"You are joking, right? My father can't bring himself to discipline me, and my mother is even more of a pushover. If he finds out that I have befriended you he will write me a strongly worded letter reminding me that I am carrying the reputation of our family on my shoulders and all that nonsense. I'll not hear about it again," Ruth said with a laugh, her carefree demeanor helping Margaret to relax a little more as well.

"Your father sounds a lot nicer than my father was. He must not drink often," Margaret replied casually, looking down at the flowers that they were now weaving into headwear for one another. It was a skill that Ruth was quite adept in, and after about an hour of patient instruction Margaret was starting to get the hang of it.

"My father drinks, but only ever a glass or two. He also never raises his voice in front of company, but that is because he hates causing a scene that would cause people to gossip about him. When you are as important as he is, you have to be extra mindful of how people perceive you. People will use whatever sort of leverage they can get over you and will exploit any weakness," Ruth said, shaking her head. "I don't want to believe that the world is like that, though. It may be that way here in London, where everything is about who you know and what you have, but the whole world can't be that way. That's why when I become of age, I want to travel the world."

"Where would you go?" Margaret rested her hands on her lap, glancing sideways at Ruth curiously. This was the first time that they'd ever really spoken about such matters, and she was genuinely curious.

"I admit, I'm not entirely certain where I would wish to travel," Ruth replied, her eyes gazing distantly toward the sky for a moment. "I've read of so many wonderful places that I should like to think I would be able to visit them all. Just like my brother is doing," she added, her face immediately brightening at the mention of him.

"What's he like, your brother? Is he anywhere near as kind as you are?" Margaret noticed the faint blush that spread across Ruth's cheeks, the redhead ws trying hard not to look too pleased with herself.

"He is one of the sweetest brothers that anyone could have ever been blessed with. He has doted on me ever since I was a babe, and goes out of his way to send me letters and little souvenirs from his travels," she said, tapping the book that sat next to Margaret. "He was the one who sent me this book. I think that you could benefit from using it to practice your letters."

"Thanks," Margaret smiled, looking over at Ruth. "I just wish there could be a way that we might spend more time together. I feel so comfortable around you," she admitted, gasping when she felt Ruth's hand squeeze hers gently.

"I have been thinking about that, and I do think I might have a solution," Ruth said, setting her completed crown of flowers onto Margaret's head. "I shall have to write to my brother and ask him if I could take you on as my personal maid. We'd get you moved in closer to me, and then we'd be able to spend more time together since you would be specifically responsible for serving me."

Margaret's mind was working furiously to try and comprehend her friend's words. *Is that kind of thing even allowed? Would Winifred ever go along with it, even if the request was coming from Ruth's family? I can already hear her accusations about me tricking Ruth into befriending me, and this would only make her more suspicious.* "I doubt Winifred would be too happy about me suddenly jumping ship."

"Does Winifred treat you well enough that you'd honestly harbour reservations about leaving her employ?" Ruth asked, the sharpness of her tone making Meg wince. "I know you only took a job with her so that you could keep yourself off the streets, but I am offering you something more. The maids in my household are all well taken care of, and I want to make sure you are similarly taken care of. Besides, when school is not in session we would have a bunch of free time together. There are so many wonderful things that I could show you. You could be like the sister I've always wanted." Ruth sounded so certain about everything that Margaret couldn't stop her heart from fluttering in her chest. Her friend made it all sound so easy, and Margaret didn't want to dash her own hopes by ruminating on her reservations. She would just have to put her faith in her friend and deal with whatever life threw at her. As long as Ruth was there with her, Margaret felt like she'd be able to handle anything.

"Could you tell me a little more about your family, Meg? I know that you have been rather tight-lipped about your origins. I promise you that I don't ask with some nefarious purpose in mind. I want to know your situation so that I can have a better idea of how I can help you get to where you ought to be," Ruth assured her, patting the top of Margaret's hand lightly.

Margaret took a deep breath, gazing up at the sky quietly for a while. When she began to speak, her voice was just loud enough that Ruth could hear her. "It all started out so normally. Daddy was a day labourer at one of the coal mines, and my mother made spare money by babysitting. We weren't living like royalty by any means, but we were content. We could have meat at least once a week, and Mother would often repair old dresses she found to keep us clothed. It was a simple life, and we seemed to be happy together."

When Ruth made no indication of interrupting, Margaret continued. "My father never used to drink, and he would take his spare money so we could go for walks in the park and occasionally get something from the street merchants. I never heard him and my mother argue either, and for the longest time I was convinced that we would just live happily like a family forever. Then my father lost his job, and everything seemed to change. He started spending more time in the bars gambling, trying to swindle the money for our expenses out of the drunkards there. Roughly two months after he lost his job, my mother died, and from then on, my father just got worse and worse." Margaret bit her bottom lip, her eyes welling up with tears.

"I'm so sorry. Meg"

Silence had sat between them for about five minutes before Margaret finally spoke again. "He used to say that Jack The Ripper had attacked her as she was coming home. Simply a lie. A lie he told so many times I think he started to believe it himself. Whenever I would try and correct him, he would get so angry. He would fly into a rage. He had a terrible temper when he was in his cups, and he had been arrested more than once for causing brawls in the nearby pubs."

"That sounds so awful." Ruth said, sounding as disappointed as Margaret felt.

"I can still feel a fear about him getting angry and hurting me again, even though he's passed on now," Margaret replied, scratching the back of her head in irritation. "Since I have been cut off from my past and my lineage, I guess I have no other option than to try and carve out a living for myself."

"I'd like to help you get to that point," Ruth replied eagerly, rising to her feet and spinning around in a circle before pointing at Margaret. "We are going to get your life back on track."

Margaret giggled at that, beaming at her friend. "I think my life is already going to be significantly better than it would have been just for knowing you."

"You flatter me, Margaret Wilshire," Ruth curtsied mischievously to her friend, sticking her tongue out playfully. "I hope I can look forward to your friendship for a long time."

"That makes two of us, Ruth."

Margaret sat together with Ruth that night as Ruth penned the letter to her brother. She didn't tell him everything per Margaret's request, but she figured she had included enough to convey the importance of the matter. Ruth assured her countless times that her brother would see no reason to prevent Margaret from joining their household, particularly when she was the one asking it of him. It would take a couple of weeks for the mail to return, Margaret waiting eagerly each day with the hope that the day would arrive that Ruth's brother would return her letter.

Winifred surprised Margaret by visiting the kitchen roughly a week and two days after they had mailed out the letter. The young maid had been in the middle of washing dishes when the sound of someone softly clearing their throat made her look up from the sink. Winifred was standing there in a neat blue dress and petticoat, an umbrella hanging from her arm. Margaret could see moisture dripping off the umbrella onto the stone floor of the kitchen. The Headmistress had clearly just returned from battling the rain that had been falling constantly since earlier that day.

"Good afternoon, Margaret. Would you be so kind as to prepare some tea for me? I got caught out in the rain and would like a chance to warm myself." Winifred's voice was surprisingly jovial and polite, her mouth tugged upward in a smile of seemingly genuine humor. "Besides, you and I need to have a little chat."

The change in attitude that the older woman displayed toward her alarmed Margaret. There was a knowing look in her eyes, but Margaret couldn't begin to wonder how the Headmistress would have gotten wind of what was going on. *Unless Shirley told her about how Ruth and I have been spending more time together, and she is here to try and weasel information out of me by playing nice. I'm onto her little game.*

"I can certainly prepare some tea, Headmistress. Please make yourself comfortable while I get everything ready," Margaret said, fetching the tea kettle and filling it with water before leaving it to boil on the stove top. She grabbed the small jar where they kept the tea leaves and set it on the small wooden stool next to her, humming to herself to try and alleviate the anxiety the Headmistress was giving her. They had barely seen one another since the first day that Margaret had been hired, so why the sudden visit now? "And for what reason have I the pleasure of your visit?"

"I wished to come down and tell you personally about the news that I just received," Winifred said, the forced sweetness in her tone doing little to fool Margaret. The older woman was very angry, and she had a feeling she knew why. "It seems that you have been making quite a good impression on one of the students here."

"I have, Ma'am?" Margaret had to bite her bottom lip to keep herself from smiling. Doing her best to keep a straight face as she turned to face the headmistress. "Why do you say that?"

"I just received a letter from Timothy Braddock; he is the elder brother of one Ruth Braddock. Since her parent's untimely passing, he makes all the decisions concerning Ruth." Winifred continued, her umbrella now held in front of her like she normally held her cane, both hands resting atop its handle. "I figured you would want to be made aware that he has officially requested that you become one of their family's private maids. You are to be moved next to the Lady Braddock's room, and you will answer specifically to her about your duties. However, keep in mind that you are still technically employed by the school. So you still answer to me, as well." The threat was plain despite Winifred's polite tone, Margaret swallowing dryly before nodding.

"I will remember, Madame Boynton," Margaret replied respectfully. The high pitched whistle of the kettle as it began to boil provided Margaret with the excuse she needed to turn her gaze from the Headmistress. "I am very grateful for everything that you have done for me so far."

"I'm happy to hear that. Hopefully that gratitude also translates into loyalty," Winifred stepped forward to take the cup that Margaret now held out for her, the fragrant scent of the warm tea filling the maid's nose until the Headmistress plucked the cup from her grasp. "Thank you for the tea," she added brusquely, exiting as quickly as she had come.

That was definitely one of the strangest conversations I have had. She looked as though she was doing her best to not be sick when she told me that Ruth's brother had written her. We've been waiting for her brother's response, but I had thought he would write back to Ruth first before talking to the Headmistress. Though, if what Ruth said about him is true, he probably figured there was no point in drawing everything out. In the meantime, I should go get my things together.

She smiled widely, her heart soaring with joy as she practically skipped down the hallway toward the servant's quarters. Humming tunelessly, she quickly pulled her dresses and jewellery from the little nightstand that had housed them for the last few months and wrapped them into a makeshift knapsack once more. It would be sufficient for her to move her things over. She was so preoccupied that she barely heard Abigail enter.

"I'm supposed to show you to your new room," Abigail said, looking wistfully at Margaret. "It's going to feel kind of weird to have the place to myself again, I admit."

"We will still be working together, Abigail," Margaret assured her, reaching over and squeezing her hand gently. "And you'll know where to find me. Don't be a stranger, all right?"

Abigal smiled good-naturedly at that, the older woman nodding slowly. "All right."

CHAPTER 7

"All right, Meg. I want you to try reading this sentence for me," Ruth said kindly, sitting beside her on the rich girl's bed after classes one night. Now that Margaret was Ruth's personal maid, it meant that the two were getting much more time to spend together despite Margaret's relatively full schedule. Her friend was convinced that Margaret would be able to accomplish her duties far more successfully if she were to be educated, and had taken it upon herself to give her young new maid lessons. They had started with her letters, the two spending weeks together with Ruth tutoring the young maid. Much to her personal delight, Margaret found that she had little difficulty in picking up on the lessons.

Most of that was no doubt because of Ruth's teaching style; she had the patience of a saint, and never seemed to chide Margaret even when she made mistakes. If anything, she saw every mistake as an opportunity to go back and review, the repetition eventually starting to cement everything slowly into her mind. By the time two months had passed, Margaret had gotten a good, basic knowledge of both letters and numbers. Ruth had even gotten her to start practicing her reading by having the young maid read to her out of the daily paper. Ruth was the kind of person who enjoyed staying up to date on current events, even if Margaret found the stuffy articles of the London Times rather boring. It seemed as though most of the news coming out was either about some noble she had never heard of or was dominated by talk of trade and taxes.

"Burglary occurring at Mondelae's Jewellery believed to be the work of same thief responsible for sudden increase in robberies in London proper. Agents of Scotland Yard believe that he may be working in tandem with a group, as the times and incidents of each robbery are far too spread out to be the work of a single man. Citizens are reminded once more to keep their valuables secure upon their persons, and to avoid travelling alone at night," she read slowly, occasionally stumbling over a word but quickly correcting herself before Ruth had a chance to. "I can't believe that there could be so many thieves living in London."

"My father says that it is only natural; the lower class has never wanted to put in the necessary effort required to give themselves a better situation. I can imagine it would be easier for someone with lesser moral fiber to filch something from someone else and pawn it off rather than subject themselves to having to work to earn it themselves," Ruth said, smiling apologetically when she saw the look that briefly flashed across her friend's face. "Not that I believe you are anything like that, Meg. You are truly a cut above the rest."

"I am relieved to hear that," Margaret admitted, setting the newspaper down on the bedside table. "I just can't help but think there is more to it than that. Surely everyone would want to work if they knew that doing so would be worth their effort. However, as a person who has tried to do odd jobs before coming here, I can tell you there are many out there who would take advantage of their workers. Half of the time the pay they offered wouldn't have been enough to buy a full meal at a restaurant, let alone to pay for housing or anything else."

"Is that right?" Ruth asked, a visible frown on her face. "I didn't realize that things were like that."

"My landlord was a relatively wealthy man as well, and I've already told you the horror stories about him. He once raised our rent three times in a single year, claiming that it was to go toward a series of renovations to the property. I can assure you that no such renovations were ever made, and the next time we saw him, he had purchased himself a brand new suit. And I can assure you that the suit he purchased did not seem to be cheaply made by any stretch of the imagination. So people with money have typically been, in my experience, rather greedy and self-absorbed. You are one of the first people that I have been acquainted with who hasn't been like that," Margaret replied kindly, biting her bottom lip while worrying that her friend might take offense.

"It's probably because of my grandmother," Ruth replied softly, gazing over at a small picture that stood on the dresser across the room from her bed. A soft-cheeked woman with a beaming smile and ash-grey hair smiling out from a small oval photograph. "She only came into money after my grandfather died prematurely and left all his money and assets to her. She came from a relatively poor family herself, and my grandfather had gone against his family to court her. He was disowned at some point, but used his cunning and education to create a fortune of his own. My grandmother had worked side by side with him, so she knew the effort that went into running the business and how quickly money could disappear if one was not careful. I like to think that it is because she had to work so hard for her success that my grandmother was better able to empathize with people of the lower class."

Margaret couldn't help but smile, feeling oddly inspired by their little chat. If Ruth's grandmother had been capable of coming from lesser means and bringing herself to greatness, surely Margaret could have a chance to accomplish the same thing. *Does that mean I will have to marry myself off to some rich man just to escape my poverty? I should hardly like to think that the only way for me to get ahead in life is to have to entrust my future to a man I'll barely know.*

"You don't look like you are having particularly happy thoughts," Ruth whispered softly, her hand moving to rest on her friend's thigh gently. "I haven't gone and upset you, have I?"

"No, nothing like that," Margaret replied quickly, a small smile tugging at the corner of her mouth. "Was just thinking about some things."

"What sort of things?" Ruth reclined on the bed, her head resting against one of the many overstuffed pillows that graced the top of her bedspread.

"Well, I can't help but think how different my life has been since you came into it. I can't thank you enough for the things that you have done for me, and I would be lying if I didn't say that the happiness I feel is enough to bring tears to my eyes. After all these years of being mistreated, I can't say that I've gotten used to experiencing such kindness yet. There are times that I worry that I'll suddenly wake up and find that I was just dreaming all this," Margaret admitted, gesturing around the room. "I don't know what I would do if I had to go back to living without you, Ruth. You have been the one true friend I could rely on without hesitation."

"That saddens me, but I am also greatly honoured. You have been a wonderful companion, Meg. Your desire to learn is rivalled only by my own, and the consistent companionship that you've provided me has helped to keep me grounded. Being surrounded by the children of the upper class, you tend to become blinded by their ways. I realized when I saw you being bullied that I didn't want to be like that to people, and you have helped to keep me honest with my own feelings. I couldn't possibly begin to thank you for what you've done for me, even if you didn't know that you were. It isn't like our friendship has been only one-sided, and I don't want you to think that you've been taking advantage of me. I know I have said it before, but I wish to politely remind you. Especially since I know Winifred has probably tried to make you think otherwise," Ruth said, her gaze suddenly intense as she looked directly into Margaret's eyes.

Margaret couldn't stop herself from swallowing nervously, suddenly finding it difficult to look her friend in the eye. *Why would she say something like that? Has she overheard something from one of the other girls? Or did she talk to Winifred herself at some point when I was away from her? She wouldn't keep something like that from me, would she?*

"I can practically read your thoughts from the look on your face," Ruth said, giggling gently into her hand. "I will put your mind at ease and tell you that I have not been talking to Winifred, but I have noticed the way that your mood seems to change on certain days, which can only make me assume that you had contact with her at that point."

"Am I really that easy to read?" Margaret asked amusedly.

"Let's just say that I wouldn't recommend you getting into poker," Ruth replied, grinning widely.

Margaret pouted playfully, crossing her arms in front of her chest as she tilted her head away from her friend. "I'm not that obvious!"

"I don't think it is a negative quality to be honest," Ruth chided, giving her friend a playful smack on the arm. "I just tell you because there are people out there who would take advantage of it. You have to be able to hide your emotions sometimes, Meg. It will be the difference between success and failure. Even if you don't agree with a person, there will be times where you can't let them know that you don't agree. It might even mean the difference between life and death."

Margaret felt a chill that she couldn't explain running down her spine. "Did something happen, Ruth?"

"Not yet, but I have been having this weird feeling lately," Ruth said softly, her eyes glancing pointedly toward the door before returning her attention to Margaret. "This conversation is making me rather nervous. Would it be all right if we talked about something else?"

"Of course, I'm sorry to upset you, Ruth. Why don't you tell me a little more about your brother." Margaret said light-heartedly, silently thankful for the excuse to talk about something else. The consistent threat of the conniving headmistress was one that followed her every day, even if her new position as Ruth's maid had helped offer her a slight reprieve. "Where is your brother now?"

"I believe he said that he made a stop in Greece in his last letter. I guess he said he wanted a chance to take in the sights of the famous landmarks there like the Parthenon and such. He has always had such a fascination with the history of Greece; it was one of the few of his lessons that he didn't complain about doing. My father was so pleased with him, since it meant that my brother would unwittingly get himself involved with very profitable ventures. Timothy went so far as to teach himself Greek, and that made sure all the universities were very interested in his potential. He could have had his choice of whatever school he'd like, but he isn't sold on any of them just yet. He told my father that after three years of traveling that he would make his decision, but it has been two years since he left home and now with Father gone he mut decide what he wants to do with hs life, and I can't wait to see what he decides for himself. I know he will be wonderful, no matter what he does," Ruth finished softly, her eyes shining as she spoke about her brother.

I wish I had a sibling who could bring me as much happiness as Timothy seems to bring to Ruth. Maybe I don't understand the intensity of her feelings for him because I have no siblings of my own, but I bet I would feel the same way. "What do you want to do in the future, Ruth? What are you going to do with your life once you come of age?"

"Timothy asks me that same question all the time and I have yet to come to a satisfying decision on that. I would love to be a doctor and try to help people, but I'm afraid that with my incredibly squeamish nature and lack of consistent health I would be a poor candidate for that. I want to donate some of my fortune to help those in need, but I won't have control of the money my father set aside for me until I become of age or get a husband, and I hardly think I'm ready for a commitment like that," Ruth said merrily, giggling as she held her face in her hands, a small blush spreading across her cheeks. "But I do hope my future husband is handsome and kind."

"As do I," Margaret agreed. "With nice big muscles and long flowing hair!"

The two young ladies devolved into a fit of giggles at that point, rolling mirthfully around on the top of the bed. It was a release the likes of which Margaret had never felt before, the troubles of her past seeming so far away in that moment. All that mattered right now was that she was here with Ruth, and their friendship was as strong as a steel chain. "I wish I had a sister like you, Ruth," Margaret admitted a short while later, gazing over at her friend as they lay side by side on the bed, both staring up at the ceiling.

"You already feel like a sister to me," Ruth replied, shocking Margaret. "As much as I love my brother to death, there are things I would never be able to discuss with him because he is a man. Only womenfolk can understand the more delicate problems that other women deal with, and I would be lying if I said that I didn't wish for an older sister who could help instruct me in times when I am unsure of myself. However, you are a little like a younger sister to me, and I can't say I am not enjoying the older sister role."

"How come you get to be the older sister?" Margaret complained, giving her friend a playful shove. "I'm a month older than you!"

"Because you don't have enough of the answers to be the big sister," Ruth replied sagely, sticking her tongue playfully out at her friend. "Maybe if you had a little more experience I would let you, but for now, you are my little sister!"

Margaret feigned annoyance, but Ruth's words pleased her more than her friend could ever know. It was a reaffirmation of the joy of belonging, of being genuinely cared about for what felt like the first time in a long time. She tried to speak, but a weak sound was all that managed to escape. She felt the wetness of tears on her cheek, but it wasn't sadness that was bubbling up from within her heart right now. Ruth must have thought otherwise, sitting up and quickly grabbing a handkerchief and rubbing it across Margaret's cheeks softly.

"I haven't gone and upset you, have I?" Ruth asked, concern etched on her face as she gazed down at her maid. "If it means that much to you, I can let you be the older sister!"

Margaret laughed, the sound bubbling up from deep within as she shook her head. "No, sweet dove. I weep out of happiness for having a friend as wondrous as you are. Words cannot express how your sentiment honors me and the gratitude I have for all that you've done for me."

When Margaret finally bid Ruth goodnight and made her way to her own bedroom, she was surprised to find that the door was sitting slightly ajar. *That is curious; I could have sworn that I closed my door firmly before going over to Ruth's room. Why is it propped open like this now?*

As she peered into the darkness of her room, she could make out the faint outline of a person standing patiently next to her bed. There was the sound of a match being slid across a tinderbox, the newly lit candle now casting a small amount of white light across the room. Margaret swallowed gently as she found herself face-to-face with Winifred, a strained smile pressed firmly on the matron's face in such a way that was most unsettling. "Hello there, Marargret. I am so pleased to hear that you have been so friendly with Ruth," the woman said, the forced politeness in her tone immediately alerting Margaret to the true meaning of her words. The headmistress was not happy at all.

"I don't see what is wrong with me making a friend, especially with you having turned the entire school against me for whatever reason. I've done nothing but be good to her; I've done my workload for both you and her up until now, so why should I not allow myself the one reward that actually means something to me. She has treated me better than anyone else, and I would sooner die than to see you come between us," Margaret said, surprised at the brazenness of her own words.

"You spend a little time with a high-society girl and you have the gall to think that you can speak to me as if I am an inferior? You need to remember your place, street urchin. You come from nothing and are nothing but a scullery maid. It is by my good graces that you remain here, and it is only my acceptance and good mood that has allowed you to spend as much time with her as you have. However, make no mistake when I say that I will not hesitate to bring this little fantasy of yours crashing back down to reality. Because no matter how long you pretend to play a princess, you'll always be nothing but a thief. You have no place with her," Winifred said softly, her words stabbing into Margaret like icy hot knives.

"I hardly think that is your place to say," Margaret replied coldly, moving toward her bed and laying across it while casting an unmistakable look of annoyance toward the Headmistress. The woman who had filled her with so much fear and shame when she had first come to the school was a stark contrast to the wonderfully patient and soft-spoken way that Ruth tended to communicate with her. "Now, if you will excuse me, I should like to go to bed now."

Winifred said nothing in response, her eyes glittering with silent malice as she slowly pushed herself up onto her feet and rounded Meg, a wicked smirk tugging up the corner of her mouth. "Don't get too comfortable with this new happiness of yours. I guarantee it is going to be short-lived."

The Headmistress left without another word, a cold chill running down Margaret's spine. *Did she just threaten me and Ruth? Should I talk to Ruth about this the next time I see her? If she is in trouble, I should do whatever I can to keep something terrible from happening to her. I wouldn't be able to forgive myself if something ever happened to her.* Margaret sighed as she flopped back on the comfortable mattress that had been her new nest for the last couple months and let out a drawn out sigh. She was just going to have to be more alert from now on, and look out for possible warning signs. If this was a game that was about to get deadly, she would need to take every precaution she could think of to try and protect Ruth from whatever foul plans the headmistress was trying to cook up.

When she finally managed to fall asleep a short while later, she found that she dreamed rather fitfully. She was overwhelmed with visions of shadowy figures attacking her with knives, each stabbing sensation in the dream feeling unnaturally real despite her mind knowing better. Her dreams also seemed to continue showing the death of

Ruth, the sight of her beloved friend's unnaturally pale skin and still body causing fresh tears to leak out of the corners of Margaret's eyes even in her sleep. When she awoke the next day, she hastened to go and try and tell her friend about the dreams she had the previous night, but Ruth seemed nowhere to be found. She didn't seem to be in her bedroom like Margaret had hoped she would be, her friend probably already making her way toward her morning lessons. *I shall have to try and speak with her later tonight when I see her next. I just hope I'm not too late to warn her.*

CHAPTER 8

Ruth had not gone to her lessons, it turns out. Two days went by before Margaret saw her friend again. It was two days before Christmas, and Margaret had gone to her friend's room to discover her laying in her bed. Her face was ghastly pale, and there were rings beneath her eyes that made her look far older. Margaret gasped, rushing over to her friend's bedside and kneeling beside her. "Ruth, you look absolutely awful! What has happened to you?"

Ruth's dry lips moved up into a small smile, but the grimace of pain never left her face. "I think something terrible has happened, Meg. I have not felt well for the last few days, and I fear that my health is only going to continue to diminish. I feel as though there is a flame within my very gut that cannot be relieved, and I am constantly suffering through intense bouts of sickness. I feel as though my head is burning up, and it is hard to move."

Margaret could only gaze down at her friend in disbelief, tears slowly starting to leak down the corner of her eyes. "Oh, sweet Ruth. Have you seen a doctor?"

"I fear there will be nothing that they can do at this point," Ruth admitted, a tear leaking down her own face. "Even now, I can feel that my time with you is limited. So, there are some things I must tell you before I pass."

"No, please don't say that. I can go get a doctor for you. They could cure you," Margaret was in full denial now, her hands moving to clasp her friend's hand. She swallowed as she felt how cold and clammy Ruth's hands felt, like she was already one foot in the grave.

"And by the time you returned, I would be long gone. No, Meg, you must stay here with me. I am afraid," Ruth said softly, her voice finally starting to quiver. "The only comfort I have right now is knowing that you are here with me in my last moments. I can't begin to apologize for the promises I will have to break to you. We won't be able to have tea with our husbands together like we planned."

Margaret was sobbing freely now, the fear that she had been harbouring within herself for months bubbling to the forefront of her mind like lava from a volcano. How could Ruth have suddenly fallen ill? *It has to have been Winifred. I don't know how she did it, but that spiteful old woman is the only one who would do something like this. I should tell someone.*

"Timothy's last letter told me that he was coming into the city for Christmas, but I fear I will not be able to meet him. I want you to find him instead, and tell him of what has happened. In my top dresser drawer you will find a letter that contains a picture of him. I need you to hide it upon your person, but take care that it not be damaged. It may prove to be the only thing that will help you once I am gone. I have told him all about you, so he will recognize you when you approach him and mention my name. He will help take care of you, now that I cannot. I know it is going to be frightening, but you have to stay strong now," Ruth said, turning her head away and coughing violently.

"I can't imagine having to live without you," Margaret replied, her heart sinking in her chest.

"I will always be with you in your heart, my sweetling. I know you will feel lonely at times, but that will only be temporary. You'll be back to feeling happiness again in no time," Ruth said, her hand moving to slide beneath her pillow for a brief moment and reappearing with a small purse that jingled with coins. "Take this. It is all of the money that I have with me. I was saving it for my first trip to France, but I won't be needing it anymore."

"I wish I had the time to pay you back for everything you've done for me," Margaret sobbed, her hands moving up to wipe the tears from her eyes. No matter how hard she tried, she just couldn't seem to stem the flood of tears. "You've been the best friend I could have asked for."

"I love you, Meg. I've loved you like a sister, and it does my heart comfort to know that you're with me. If you wouldn't mind, could you promise me one last thing before I go? I want you to try and continue practicing your lessons. The money I have left you should be more than enough to find yourself sufficient lodgings until you can get in contact with Timothy. I can't imagine what horrible things you may have to experience in the aftermath of my passing, but just know that our Lord brought you into my life for a reason. You will be saved from this life of misery one day, Meg. Just survive until then, no matter what you must do," Ruth reached out and grabbed Meg's hand tightly as she spoke, the remnants of the vigor that Margaret was used to seeing in her eyes flashed briefly.

Margaret hung her head, unable to shed any more tears. She felt exhausted and numb all at the same time, the knowledge that these were the last few moments she would ever have with her best friend making it hard for her to speak. "Ruth, if there is anything else that you need to tell me, do so now. I need you to tell me everything that you remember. When did you notice that you were feeling ill?"

"Two days ago," Ruth replied softly, looking up at her. "It

started when you served me that roast dinner on Tuesday."

"Do you think that it might just be that an undercooked morsel of food is making you sick?" Margaret asked, hoping that their fears were being overblown.

"I thought that at first, but there was something strange about the way it tasted, not the way it was cooked. It looked fully done to me, but when I was eating it there was a bitter taste that I couldn't figure out the source of. I thought maybe one of the spices had soured, but the meal that I had the following day had the same taste," Ruth's expression was wistful, looking at Margaret with slightly narrowed eyes.

Margaret could feel bile rising in the back of her throat as her friend spoke, suspicions wriggling now in the back of her mind like a nest full of worms. "Impossible. You don't think that someone had you poisoned, do you?" She had heard about such things happening countless times in the stories her mother used to read to her, but she had no way of knowing what the usual signs were.

"That is not outside the realm of possibility," Ruth said softly, taking in a ragged breath before continuing. "And if that is what happened, then all the more reason why you must tell Timothy what happened. No matter what terrible things she might do to slander your name, do not ever believe that you are responsible for this. I know you love me too much to have been the one to poison me, and that is a truth that God knows. No one will ever be able to change that"

Margaret squeezed her friend's hand gently, not knowing what else to say. "I will name my daughter after you one day. I only pray that she is half as beautiful in body and soul as you have proven to be."

"You would name your child after me?" Tears streamed slowly down Ruth's cheeks again, the sick girl hiccuping gently. "You have blessed me in a way that you could never know."

"Is there anything else I can do for you, Ruth? Before it is too late?" Margaret asked softly, grabbing a washcloth from the bedside table and gently wiping away the sweat that had accumulated on Ruth's forehead.

"Can you sing that song you used to sing?" Ruth's smile was warm, though the light in her eyes seemed to be slowly fading. "I did so love hearing it; let it serve as the last song I hear to carry me on my way."

Margaret choked back a sob; she had learned the song from her mother back when she was just a young girl, and it was one of the few keepsakes she still had from those days. Ruth had been adamant on learning it, and they'd almost gotten the first two verses memorized. "Are you going to try to sing along?"

"For the parts I remember, definitely," Ruth affirmed, her body racked by a coughing fit shortly afterward.

Margaret began to sing softly, the faint sound of her friend's voice accompanying her. The song was admittedly helping Margaret feel just slightly better, at least until she heard Ruth take one last rattling breath before going completely still. As she finished the last line of the song, Margaret rested her head gently on her friend's chest and wept. Once again, she was all alone.

CHAPTER 9

Margaret only had enough time to conceal the coin purse and Ruth's letter in the inner folds of her uniform before the door to Ruth's bedroom was flung open, a smug look of triumph on Winifred's face. The headmistress's shadow loomed across Margaret's face, the young maid doing everything in her power to contain the rage that suddenly swelled within her. The older woman was surprisingly dressed up, looking like she was about to go attend one of the high-class parties that were favored by the upper crust.

"What have you done to poor Ruth?" Winifred asked softly, her voice filled with the same kind of false kindness that she always displayed when it came to Margaret. "How could you have poisoned your best friend?"

"I would never poison her," Margaret snarled, her eyes seething with hatred as she glared back at the headmistress. "Even she knew as much. You might be interested in knowing, however, that she suspected you all along."

"Is that so?" Winifred crossed the room in a matter of moments, her ironclad grip squeezing down around Margaret's wrist and causing a squeal of pain to escape her. "I can't imagine why you girls would dare accuse someone like me of such a thing, but I can guarantee you that this is entirely on your own head. If you had just stayed a good little maid and kept your head down, poor Ruth would still be around. Instead, you poisoned her with your inferiority and led to her death. I wouldn't be surprised if she caught some commoner's disease off you."

"The only sickness around here is the one in your head," Margaret growled, her words being met with a powerful backhand smack from the matronly woman across her cheek. Pain lanced through her jaw, the blow containing more force than even her father had ever used on her. Fighting back the pain, Margaret made sure to keep her gaze focused on Winifred. "I don't care if you hit me. That won't change the fact that you are a murderer, and I will make sure that everyone discovers what you did. Even if it is the last thing I ever do!"

"Even if you told anyone, it would be your word against mine. Who do you think the police would be more likely to believe? The wealthy and influential headmistress of this school, or a lowly scullery maid whose head got too big for her station?" Winifred's eyes were drilling into

Margaret now, a smug smile telling the young maid that the headmistress already knew the answer to her own question.

"You think you are so clever. That you have somehow risen above the rest of us because of where you happen to work. Well, I'll tell you this, Winifred. I was a wonderful friend to Ruth, and she was to me. And with all the letters she wrote her brother, he knows as well. All I have to do is tell him what terrible thing you have done, and he will help me bring the hand of justice right down upon your head!" Margaret wrenched her hand away from Winifred's grip, feeling the powerful sting of the headmistress's hand across her cheek.

She clutched her mouth as red-hot pain flooded her cheek, her eyes welling up with tears even as she fixed her gaze on the vindictive old woman before her. There was a look on the old woman's face that sent a shudder of loathing through Margaret. Winifred was chuckling softly now, the sound more terrible than any that the young maid had heard from her before. "You would bring me down, is that right? You think that an insignificant speck like you would be capable of doing anything against me? Tonight I will mail out a letter to Ruth's brother letting him know of her demise, and make no mistake that I will tell him that you poisoned her."

Winifred's cane moved in a quick flash, smacking across Margaret's mid section with enough force to knock the wind out of her. She gripped her stomach as she doubled over, coughing up blood onto the wooden floor. She felt Winifred's grip on her hair, screeching in pain as she was roughly yanked to her feet.

"However, I can't risk for a moment that you go spouting off to the wrong people. I have to think about not only myself, but the wonderful girls here at my school," Winifred said, her words causing Margaret to scoff. Her insubordination was met with a rough tug on her hair, the headmistress now pulling Margaret bodily toward the exit to Ruth's room. Margaret was not going to go without a fight, however, and made sure to kick and scream as they went. She tried to claw at Winifred's hands, but the old woman simply punched her each time until Margaret couldn't bring herself to keep struggling.

Winifred led her to the kitchen, moving past the familiar stove toward the door to the cellar. Margaret's fear intensified, memories of the darkness of the cellar from times when she had been forced to go down to retrieve ingredients flooding her thoughts. She had never done well with dark places, especially if there was the chance of her being trapped within it. As Winifred pushed her forward toward the small crawl space under the cellar steps, Margaret's efforts to escape intensified. She did her best to yank herself away from Winifred, only to be tripped by the older woman. She felt her wrist being released, but without being able to catch herself in time she could only throw up her hands to protect her head as she crashed into the tiny room.

"I hope that you enjoy this time here. I will be taking my time to pen the letter to Ruth's brother, and once that is finished I will be alerting the police about what you did. In the meantime, trapping you here will mean that you won't be able to run off and try and railroad me. I hope that you enjoy your time down here in isolation; It will be the last bit of solitude you get before they carry you off to prison. Assuming that you don't hang for killing the daughter of a very rich nobleman," Winifred cackled in glee, shutting the small door to the crawl space and sliding the lock into place, cackling as she listened to Margaret banging desperately on the door.

"No! No! No!" Margaret kept hammering her hands in desperation upon the wooden frame of the door, hopelessness welling up within her as she realized that the door had yet to give an inch.

"Goodbye, Thief. I would say that it was a pleasure knowing you, but I will be sleeping better at night knowing that you are gone. Maybe the stench of your poorness will eventually begin to fade, given enough time," Winifred said, laughing as she slowly moved toward the cellar doors. "Enjoy the few hours you have left. I suppose it was a good run, but I should have known that you would only be a temporary fixture here. After all, you just weren't born with the right stuff."

The sound of the cellar doors being slammed closed soon followed, plunging the room into complete darkness. Margaret huddled down in the cramped space and gripped her knees, tears rolling down her face. She wept for Ruth and all that her friend would not be able to do, and for herself for how powerless she was in this situation. *She thinks she is so smart, but I will show her. This silly little door won't hold me for long. If I have to dig my out of here with my bare hands, I will escape.*

Margaret allowed her hands to slowly travel along the doorframe, trying to get a gauge of it in the lack of light. She blinked gently, straining her eyes to be able to make out even the faintest detail. If she could just find out where the mechanism for the lock was, perhaps she could focus her attention on that spot. *The coins! Maybe I can use one of them to help me.* She reached down into her brassiere and fished one of the metal coins out of the coin purse Ruth had given her.

The coin felt cool and sturdy in her hand, the young girl gritting her teeth as she set about trying to pry at the door. She let out a faint groan each time her fingernails scraped on the wooden door, the pain causing her to hesitate briefly at each moment. Only her determination and desire to escape helped to fuel her enough to continue. *You think that you have me beat? Just you wait until I manage to get out of here. I will go straight to the police. Hopefully you won't have had enough time to get in contact with an officer; because otherwise I'll be spending the majority of my time trying to avoid the police, and that will make finding Timothy much more difficult.*

Her vision blurred with bitter tears, biting her bottom lip hard enough that blood began to trickle down her jaw. She hated that she had to go through something like this when she should be focused on grieving for her friend.

She sighed in irritation as the tips of her fingers soon grew too sore for her to continue for the moment, her breathing laboured as she gently nursed her hands against her body. They felt as though a bright flame was coursing through the tips of them, and it was hard for her to keep a grip on the coin now that her fingers were swollen. *It hurts! Mommy it hurts too much for me to do this!* Tears streamed down her face as she knelt on the floor, the coin falling onto the hem of her skirt as her fingers suddenly spasmed and lost their grip. She closed her eyes and sobbed bitterly, the pain in her fingers throbbing unceasingly for the poor girl. *God, please! Give me the strength to do this. I don't want to be trapped here until I'm dragged away to prison. Please give me the strength!*

Margaret's thoughts quickly turned to Ruth's brother: Timothy. *What if the police or the papers get word to Timothy before I do? They will all be convinced that I am the wrongdoer because Winifred will spin the yarn to make me the guilty party!*

The thought alone was enough to cause Margaret to slowly start climbing to her feet, gripping the coin clumsily in her swollen fingers and renewing her efforts at it. It looked as though her constant worrying had managed to chip away enough of the wood that she could almost feel the coin dig against the lock as she scraped against the door. *Just a little more. Just a little more and I will be able to start making my escape.*

After what felt like hours in the darkness, Margaret finally heard the loud click of the lock disengaging. She slammed her foot into the center of the door, feeling a smug satisfaction as she felt it swing outward. She crawled through the small gap the door provided, pressing the coin back into her brassiere and shivered at the feeling of the cold metal against her flesh. But there was something else; something sticky and warm that she couldn't quite identify. As she felt the first wooden step and began climbing, she felt her resolve hardening with every step. *I hope you are prepared, Winifred. I've managed to gain my freedom, and once I've escaped the school grounds I am going to bring you down.* As she pushed the door open, she smiled in triumph. The expression faded quickly though, as she found herself face to face with the woman who had replaced Abigail as head cook a few months ago. Her name was Bertha, and she was every bit as nasty as Winifred was.

CHAPTER 10

"Oh, and what do we have here?" The large woman with permanently flushed cheeks was sitting in her rocking chair, peeling potatoes diligently with a sizable chef's knife gripped dexterously in her hand. She immediately stabbed her knife into the cutting board beside her, the half-peeled potato being dropped carelessly back into the basket that sat at her side. "I see that the desperate little mouse has managed to free itself from the cage. I admit, I didn't believe you would be able to get out. I told the headmistress that any fool desperate enough to get out of that door could, but I can also guess you didn't manage it through your own strength. Tell me, what did you use to get free?"

Margaret didn't immediately answer. Instead, she moved over to where a loaf of bread sat cooling and lifted it up. She bit into the end of the loaf with no fear of repercussions, her mind made up. The headmistress had punished her for taking a single piece of bread once, so this time, she was going to get the whole loaf. Better for her to know that she would be punished for something worthwhile this time should she find herself caught.

"Have you lost your mind?" Bertha asked, watching Margaret's actions with total disbelief. "You know that you don't get to eat anything but the scraps."

Margaret looked at Bertha like the cook was crazy. "From this moment onward, I don't work for this place anymore. The headmistress has violated our agreement countless times, and her sins couldn't begin to be compared to me taking a single loaf of bread."

"And what exactly is to stop me from going and raising the alarm? Last I heard, you were nothing but a lowly orphan the headmistress allowed to work here. I doubt you have the money to pay for that loaf of bread you are eating, let alone enough to find yourself a place to stay on such short notice," Bertha replied triumphantly, pointing her sausage-thick finger at Margaret with a gleeful smile. "A thief to the end, I see."

Margaret's jaw clenched as she silently reached into her brassiere and pulled out a clean coin, holding it up for Bertha to see. The portly woman gasped, her pig-like face immediately twisting in a greedy smile. "Oh, so that is how it is. You used a coin to scrape the wood away. I'll have to remember to get better wood on that door in the future. I guess going the cheap route really does cost you more in the end. However, I wouldn't just let you get away from here for nothing. You better hope that you have five of those coins to part with if you hope to walk out of here without me alerting Winifred to your escape until you have enough time to get away."

Margaret swallowed angrily but immediately reached back into her brassiere, feeling cheated as she felt for four more of the highly valuable coins and dropped the requested number onto the fat woman's outstretched palm. Bertha quickly pulled her hand back toward herself and slid it into the pocket of her apron, the coins jingling softly as the cook waddled back to her chair and took a seat once more. The wooden chair creaked ominously under the woman's girth but seemed to be holding.

"Good girl; I'm glad that you aren't too stupid to know when you have been outsmarted. Now get along before I change my mind and turn you into the headmistress anyway. Last I heard from her, she was getting in contact with the funeral parlour to send a mortician. I know she sent a runner, so I imagine they will be by any time now. I wouldn't linger too much longer, little mouse. And you can't afford to be found out, can you? After all, you poisoned that poor Braddock girl," Bertha said, her eyes gleaming darkly.

There were a thousand replies that Margaret could have used in that instant, but she remembered Ruth's words. *Sometimes, the best thing to say is nothing. It guarantees no miscommunication and can speak volumes over shouting like a common drunkard. There will be people on whom your words are wasted. Concentrate on the task at hand and do not let yourself be distracted.*

Taking a deep breath, Margaret moved her bloody hands to the hem of her skirt and started making her way toward the back entrance. She didn't cast a single backward glance at the school that had served as her home for the last six months, but the chill of the December air as she stepped out caused her to shiver. *I wish I could grab some clothing or something, but that will have to wait for now. I need to get as far away from here as possible.*

Her breathing was labored as she took off at a sprint, the hungry girl still gripping the loaf of bread in her hand like it was a prize. She rounded the school and came to a screeching halt at the sign of the bobbies that were standing in front of the school. Winifred was with them, the older woman gesturing wildly as she spoke. No doubt she was already filling the officer's heads with horrible lies about her. Margaret wanted to shout at Winifred; to call her a lying snake in front of everyone. To do so would get their attention on her, and that wasn't something that would be good for her. The time for her to set things straight with the police would come later, but for now, she needed to keep going, Turning her back on the direction of Winifred and the bobbies, Margaret cut down a side street.

There was no one else out this late in this part of town; most self-respecting citizens would have been tucked away in their beds at this hour of night. Margaret exhaled warm breath onto her hands, noticing for the first time just how bad they looked. A few of her nails were so broken that the red flesh beneath was exposed, blood dripping slowly down onto the ground below her. Her fingers were purple and red, with the dried blood making it hard to tell if she was still bleeding or not. She considered it almost a blessing that she couldn't feel the chill in her fingers, but the sensation wouldn't last for long.

There was a faint sheathe of snow that had begun falling, the cold snowflakes instantly melting when they came in contact with her warm flesh. As they ran down her face, it would look for a moment as if she were crying. *Now it seems as though God is either mocking me or trying to cry for me. I can't quite decide which one yet. However, the important thing for right now is to find a quiet, out of the way place that I can hide out.*

She was tempted to try and stay by one of the nearby bridges, but she figured that would be one of the first places they would search for her. No, she would need to think far more carefully. Her mind wandered to Timothy, a faint blush managing to spread across her cheeks as the image of him in the photograph flashed through his mind. He had been remarkably handsome, his short cut hair stopping just past his eyes. The bangs were swept away from a wide forehead, but his eyes were warm and cheerful, a good match to the wide smile that showed off his straight, clean teeth. He seemed to be dressed in a brown suit, though the black and white photograph made it so he could just as easily have been dressed in black. His white shirt peeked out from beneath the lapel of his suit jacket, the absence of the tie striking Margaret as a little odd. Most gentlemen she knew insisted on wearing some kind of tie, even if only a bow tie.

Ruth did say that he was a bit different than the other boys his age. Maybe it is just another one of his particular quirks. Like the way he will only drink tea that has had the juice of a freshly squeezed orange added to it. She shook her head to try and dispel thoughts of him for now. It wouldn't do for her to let her mind wander right now when she was out in public and easily recognizable. The police would have slowly started spreading Winifred's report by now, and they would be on the lookout for the girl with the birthmark who had poisoned a student. *I can't help but feel angry that the police will take her word at face value. It must be nice to be able to pay your way out of following the rules.*

Margaret stepped into a side street quickly when she heard the sound of a man shouting in the distance, a quick glance affording her a view of the uniformed man standing at the far end of the street. She pressed her body up against the cool bricks behind her, the chill managing to seep into her skin even through the clothing she wore. She wished she had a map of some kind, and that she knew how to read a map. It was one of the lessons that she and Ruth had been preparing to begin before Winifred had poisoned her. *Where did Ruth say that her brother would be staying? It had the name of an animal in it, right?*

She crept slowly through the dark alleyway, her heart hammering steadily in her chest as she gazed around frantically. Her eyes were straining to catch even the faintest bit of light. She worried that she might run into some evil vagrant or cutpurse, grateful that she had temporarily chosen to keep it tucked in her brassiere's inner recesses. No one would think that she would hide it in such a place, and that would help her hold onto her coins that much longer.

"I guess that the first thing I could do is try to find a room to be posted up in for a couple of days," she muttered to herself, the rumbling in her stomach, causing her to cast a sullen glance at the half-crushed loaf of bread in her hand. *To think that I was almost looking forward to dinner tonight. Probably for the best that I didn't take anything but this bread. Lord knows she probably would have tried to poison me as well should her plan with the police fail.*

Stepping out of the alley brought with it fresh air, the smell of refuse and stale waste being replaced by that of cooking food and flowers from the nearby flower shop. Margaret admired the bright red roses that sat upright and strong in the display. A moment of longing struck through her, her eyes closing as she took a deep inhalation of the scent. It reminded her of the smell of Ruth's perfume. *If every little thing I come across is going to remind me of her, the upcoming days are going to be quite hard on me.*

"Excuse me, little missus. You look like you are unaccompanied and needing some cheering up. How would you like to spend the night with good old Maxwell Clark," said a thickly accented voice from behind her. She gazed passively over the shoulder, taking in the sight of a rather well-dressed young man whose suit jacket looked faintly dirty, like he'd been wearing it for a while. His skin was slightly tanned, like he spent a majority of his day out in the sun. She wondered if he was one of the labourers, but his dress seemed far too nice for him to be just a lowly worker.

"I'm sorry sir, but I will have to pass. I am afraid that I merely took a wrong turn, but I have my bearings once more. Thank you for your kind concern," she replied, curtsying as best as she could before racing away from him, leaving the confused young man where he stood.

CHAPTER 11

Margaret wasn't sure how she had managed it, but she found a week had gone by without any interaction between her and the police. She had been careful to use a fake name wherever she went, and was mindful to face the shopkeepers in such a way that her birthmark wasn't visible to them. She didn't want to catch flack from any of them about being a witch or any other such nonsense, and she definitely didn't want people to see it if the police had it included in her description.

She'd bought one of the newspapers from a young boy standing in front of the Inn, in which she had rented a room for the night to get out of the rain, her lack of luggage making it easy for her to hop from place to place without raising too much suspicion. She was pleased that the thriftiness she was using while spending was helping stretch out her money, but it wouldn't last forever. The memory of the confrontation with Sly was still fresh in her mind, and she found herself sometimes awakening to night terrors involving the wrathful man finding her again. It had been different when she was safely hidden within the walls of the boarding school, but now that she would be traipsing across London, that left her exposed.

She'd slowly started making her way toward the East End of London, figuring that she might be able to find an out of the way park where she could hunker down for a while. She'd heard plenty of rumors about the tendency of homeless persons to congregate in the parks, and the bobbies had gotten so frustrated with constantly trying to remove them that they practically stopped bothering to try and remove them. *If I can manage not to get robbed, I'll be sitting pretty well for a while. They wouldn't bother trying to look all around town to try and find me, would they?*

She tucked the newspaper under her arm as she set off down the road, her nose once again bombarded by the myriad smells that wafted through the London air. She could smell fresh cooked meat from one of the nearby restaurants, the cooks no doubt preparing for the mid-afternoon lunch rush. The mouthwatering scents of shepherd's pie, fish and chips, and pastries all merged in the air to create a symphony of temptation. *It would be nice to be able to enjoy a nice, warm meal for once. Perhaps I could treat myself just once to a hot plate. It won't kill me to enjoy something.*

She stopped outside of Simpson's-In-The-Strand, a rather well-known establishment whose humble beginnings as a coffee house had soon evolved as one of the best known places in London to have a meal and a game of chess. The distinct smell of a Sunday Roast assaulted her nose, the promise of warm beef in her stomach causing the hungry young woman to practically float through the front doors. She easily weaved past the various patrons, making her way to an unoccupied table she had spotted as she came in through the door. There was a group of older men sitting to her right, two of them seemingly embroiled in a very heated match of chess. One of them was a very thin man with a flowing white beard that hung well past his belt, his eyes squinted deeply as he peered in a nearsighted manner down at his pieces, his tongue occasionally swiping across his lips in agitation.

"Welcome to Simpson's-In-The-Strand, known throughout all of Europe. Our specials tonight are a Sunday Roast or our nationally enjoyed Fish and Chips. Do you know what you'd like, or can I give you a moment to look over the menu?" The question came from a cheerful looking young girl in an outfit similar to Margaret's, albeit far cleaner. She had piercing blue eyes and long golden hair that hung past her shoulders in graceful rivulets. Margaret swallowed gently as she kept her face slightly averted from the serving girl.

"Can I get the cheapest hot item on your menu? I don't have much coin to spend, but would very much appreciate something nice and warm in my belly. Times have been relatively hard on me, and having something warm might serve to boost my spirits," Margaret replied, her eyes moving to rest fleetingly on the serving girl's face. The smile that she wore seemed to be genuine, but Margaret could almost feel the girl's judgment in her gaze, suddenly feeling very self-conscious that she hadn't tried to find somewhere to wash up before arriving.

"Pinching your pennies right now, eh? Nothing wrong with that. My grandfather says people have a tendency to let their coin slip through their fingers too quickly when it comes to purchasing things they don't need. Better to live smart then to make yourself poor in a night, that's what he used to say. Can't tell you if that was him genuinely learning his lesson or just getting tired of getting shaken down for his gambling debts," the blonde said with a laugh, her hand held in front of her mouth respectfully. "However, if you are looking for something nice and hot but cheap, I know exactly what you want."

She gently curtsied before moving away from Margaret, leaving the young girl to gaze around the restaurant absently while she waited for her food. She sipped daintily from the glass of water that had been brought to her when the serving girl had first approached, the coolness of it soothing her parched throat. She hadn't managed to get a drink for over half a day, not wanting to risk the various public places that offered it for fear of being found by the police. She hadn't thought to ask one of the shopkeepers for a glass of water, since such kindness was unheard of in her part of the slums, and she somewhat doubted that the upper class was any more generous. *Ruth had been; she was one of the few, but she showed me that there is just as much capacity for kindness as there is cruelty in the hearts of people. I used to believe that when Mother was around; maybe I can start to believe it again?*

Margaret found her thoughts were interrupted by the return of the serving girl, carrying a large wooden plate from which one of the most heavenly aromas was emanating. Memories of the rare Sunday evenings when they could afford meat and potatoes rushed back to the forefront of her mind at the sight of the slices of roast beef sitting atop a mountain of mashed potatoes with a thick, rich brown gravy poured all atop it. When her mother and father had worked together to cook it, they had always presented it like it was a veritable feast.

"Thanks for waiting. This roast was part of the last batch that was cooked, so it isn't quite as fresh. I figured this way we won't have to charge you too much for it. Don't let my papa know that I'm giving it to you cheap, though," she said, offering Margaret a playful wink before casting a cautionary glance back in the direction of the kitchen. "Just make sure you settle your bill with me, all right? My name is Holly."

"Thank you, Holly. I will keep that in mind," Margaret replied, watching the serving girl bounce skip away before returning her attention back to the plate now sitting before her. Her stomach rumbled once more, goading her into picking up her knife and fork and slowly slicing a thick chunk of meat away from her portion. She lifted it slowly before her, watching as the excess gravy dropped back down onto the plate. before taking a bite of the savory meat. Tears flowed down her cheeks as she slowly chewed, taking the time to fully enjoy the various complexities of its flavor. That, and it was the first bit of warm food she had enjoyed since she had left the boarding school.

It didn't take long for her to finish her food, using a small piece of bread she'd been given to mop up any remnants of gravy from the plate. She felt more satisfied than she had in a long time, surprised that she'd managed to eat as much as she had. *That will be worth not having another meal like it in a long while. I will probably regret this choice when my money starts to get lower, but for now, this was the best choice ever!*

"I take it from the look on your face that you enjoyed that quite a bit," Holly said from beside her, causing Margaret to let out a little squeak of surprise. She hadn't seen her approaching. "I hate to bother you, but I wanted to warn you that there is a bobbie out front looking for a girl with a birthmark on her cheek. I told him I would come and check and asked him to wait outside, but who knows if he will actually listen to me. There is a back entrance to the restaurant, and as a favour to you, I'll show you where it is. I didn't ask why he was looking for you, but I am sure it can't be for anything good."

Margaret's stomach rolled, panic rushing through her as she quickly scooted out from her booth. She reached into her coin purse and fished a few of the larger coins out, pressing a few into Holly's hand before the blonde guided her toward the back of the restaurant, a small wooden door leading out into a dark alley. As Holly ushered Margaret out, Margaret could hear the voice of someone echoing out above the noise of the establishment. "This is the police! Everyone in the establishment, remain where you are. We are looking for a dangerous criminal who is currently on the run. Anyone with any information should cooperate, and perhaps you shall be rewarded."

Margaret pressed another few coins into Holly's hand, looking her directly in the eyes. "I was never here," she muttered, dashing away from the restaurant shortly afterward. She slowed down to a brisk walk once she had gotten a good few blocks away. She sighed gently, slumping against the nearby wall, positioning herself so she was hidden behind a sizable wall of shrubbery. She had wandered into a wealthier residential area, it seemed, but that simply meant there would be more places for her to hide. She lamented the fact that all her mother's jewellery was still hidden within her bag at the boarding school. *Unless Winifred dug through my things and stole them.*

Margaret rested her head back against the shrub behind her, finding that the leaves crackled where they had been frozen, but cradled her head well enough, if not for being a bit soggy. *It could certainly be worse; it could be raining right now. Or snowing...* She glanced up at the sky, half expecting the heavens to suddenly divulge a large amount of rain down onto her head in another one of its cosmic jokes on her. She ended up slumping down onto her side roughly an hour after falling asleep, her head resting on her upper arms as she rested fitfully, fighting back the cold. Her dreams were plagued by images of bobbies chasing after her, their voices echoing in her mind. She could hear Constable Jones' voice calling her a criminal, as well as Winifred's cruel laughter as the image of Ruth's cold body centered itself firmly in her mind. When Margaret woke up a few hours later, the sky had darkened completely and the stars were shining brightly overhead. With the absence of any man-made light around her, there was nothing to prevent her from being able to gaze up at the vast, starlit sky. Rolling gently onto her side, she did her best to ignore that her fingers had gone numb, and she eventually willed herself back to sleep.

CHAPTER 12

Another week soon passed by, though Margaret had long since lost track of what day it was. Christmas had come and gone without any indication that it had been there. *I would say that I am used to not getting anything for Christmas, but at least it used to be one of the few days of the year where Father wasn't always in a terrible mood. Even if he did spend the whole day drinking, he typically kept himself in a good mood by singing Christmas carols.*

This year, Christmas had been spent huddled miserably beneath one of the nearby bridges to stay away from the cold. A kindly older woman who had happened to spot Margaret while she was walking alone back toward her hidey hole had given Margaret a thin blanket that even now was wrapped around her body, offering a little comforting warmth against the chill breeze that consistently whipped past her.

In the aftermath of her close call with the bobbies at the restaurant, Margaret had taken to rubbing dirt and soot on her face in an attempt to cover up the telltale birthmark that easily identified her. She hated the feeling of the grime that was beginning to coat her skin, but felt it was a wonderful alternative to being jailed or hanged for a crime she didn't commit. There were times when she would break down sobbing, her heart feeling bitter over the constant mistreatment that she was forced to endure. *I wish I had some idea of where Timothy might be. That would help narrow down the places where I would have to search, since I can't risk going into multiple establishments to enquire about him.*

Being on the run, she was finding, was at the top of her list of least favorite things. Right up there with being homeless and going hungry. With her having made her way over to the East End, the smell of the nearby Thames causing her to wrinkle her nose slightly. Ship horns sounded in the distance, the faint sound of sailors shouting to one another easily audible from her current position next to Regent's Canal. Indecision was gnawing at her insides as she gently slipped her coin purse from within her brassiere and quickly counted her remaining money. After a few quick calculations, she realized with a start that she only had enough money to last another three days, if that.

She slipped her coin purse back into the pocket of her uniform, thankful for the long skirt that draped down to just above her ankles to provide a bit of protection from the bitter cold breeze wafting in from the river. If she went closer to the docks and asked one of the sailors, perhaps one of them might know about Ruth's brother. Anything had to be better than continuing to waltz around London half frozen. *It might not be the greatest plan, but it is a plan.*

"Hey there, Girlie. You look like you are indecisive about something," the gruff voice of a sailor said from close enough behind her to make her turn around. He was an older looking man; she'd guess mid-thirties to early forties by the look of him. He was dressed in the typical blue and white of the Royal Navy, though his lapel was bare of medals of any kind. His wispy moustache looked out of place on his otherwise manly features; it would have looked more fitting on a younger man only just hitting manhood.

"Just trying to decide my next place to go," she replied cheerfully, doing her best to keep her tone pleasant. There was a strange vibe coming off the man that she couldn't quite place, but she didn't want to bring more attention to herself by causing a ruckus. "I've been doing some sightseeing while hoping to run into a friend of mine."

"Oh? What is your friend's name? Perhaps I have been acquainted with them and can assist you," he offered, his hands fidgeting against one another in such a way that made Margaret slightly nervous. "I do so love to help out young damsels in distress."

Something about the way he said the word distress caused Margaret to take a step back. There was something about the way his brown eyes kept sweeping over her that made her uncomfortable.

"Do you know Timothy Braddock?" She asked hopefully, her hands gripping her skirt nervously. "He is the one I've been searching for."

"Afraid that I don't know anyone by that name. However, I'd be more than happy to keep you company while you look," he answered a little too eagerly.

"I'm afraid I'll have to politely decline, sir. I wouldn't want to trouble you with my problems, nor would I want you to go out of your way. If you will excuse me, I think I will go and continue my search now. God bless," she spoke with finality, turning on her heels to try and walk away from him. She no sooner got down the length of the bridge that she suddenly felt someone bump roughly into her. She struggled to keep her feet, feeling hands on her for the briefest instant. She assumed they were trying to steady her, everything going so quickly that she barely registered the feeling of someone's hand briefly probing around within her pocket.

"Sorry," called out a young voice. Margaret managed to catch a glimpse of a young boy who looked no older than his early teens racing away from her. Blonde hair was covered by a cap that was pulled down just enough that the brim concealed his eyes, and the speed with which he ran made it hard for her to glimpse any of his features.

"What was that all about?" Margaret muttered to herself, patting her uniform derisively to knock some of the excess dust from her. When her hand patted over her pocket, her hand froze. Her eyes spread wide in horror, glancing down at herself as she began to pat over both of her pockets frantically. The familiar weight of Ruth's coin purse was gone, along with the little bit of money she had remaining..She slowly sank down onto her knees, despair washing over her. Without her money, how was she going to feed herself?

"Now that's what I call a rotten spot of luck," the sailor said from behind, having slowly been making his way toward her in the aftermath of her collision. "If it wasn't for this bad knee of mine I could have tried to chase him down for you. I should have warned you that there were pickpockets in the area. They especially love to try and target people here on the bridge."

Sure, now you tell me. "That was all of the money I had left to my name," she said, frustrated tears slowly escaping from her eyes and flowing unchecked down her cheeks, cutting faint lines in the dust and grime that covered her face.

"That's just how it goes sometimes." The sailor smirked. "This world ain't a kind one, missy. Best get used to it. No miracles for us." He winked at her, and sauntered off, whistling out of tune as he went.

Looks like I am right back to square one. I knew I should have kept the purse better concealed! She looked up at the darkening skies, the smell of approaching rain strong on the air. *How could today possibly get any worse?*

CHAPTER 13

The rain came shortly afterward, heavy thick drops that seemed to carry all the chill of the season liquified. Margaret gasped as the first of many drops thundered down onto her, less than a minute passing before every last bit of her was soaked to the skin. She dashed up the street toward the nearest place of solace, resulting in her sitting beneath the opening of one of the nearby shops. Since everything was closed down for the night, she doubted that anyone was going to chance across her while she waited for the rain to let up. She held her face up to the rain briefly, allowing her face to be gently washed clean of some of the accumulated grime that still managed to coat her body. *Not exactly the best kind of bath, but it does make me feel slightly better.*

The sound of tuneless whistling reached Margaret's ears, the sound seeming to echo through the rain from the corner of the street. She could see a solitary figure under a large black umbrella walking through the rain, the faint thumping of boots as the figure continued on his way growing louder as he headed her way. The thick rain made it a bit hard for her to make out much on the approaching person, but the black uniform that he wore was unmistakable. Margaret's blood ran cold, and she immediately rose to her feet. She suddenly regretted having let her face be cleaned, very much self-conscious of her birthmark that could easily be seen now.

"Move along, you. You are currently occupying private property after hours, and the owner has been very clear to us that he'll not abide any loiterers," the man called out, the constant pattering of the rain making it a little hard to hear him. "It's a wet night, so don't make me have to go and exert myself. My missus will kill me if I get her sick again so soon after nursing her back to health from the last time she fell ill."

Margaret simply nodded, slowly stepping away from the porch and starting to walk in the direction of Westminster Bridge. She kept her face turned away from him, doing her best not to walk quickly to avoid rousing the officer's suspicion. She closed her eyes when she heard him call out once more. "Excuse me, may I have a quick word with you?"

"I fear that I am on my way to a prior engagement," she lied, her voice shaking in a mixture of cold and fear. "I was only trying to take shelter from the rain, but since you have asked me to move on, I shall make my way."

"I understand that, but I have some questions for you. You are dressed in the outfit of a scullery maid, and we happen to currently be looking for someone matching the description of your clothing," he said, his voice sounding far closer now. She panicked, casting her eyes backward. Whatever look she had on her face caused the officer to break into a jog toward her. Throwing all caution to the wind, Margaret turned away from him and began to run. "Hey, stop running or I shall be forced to assume you are guilty!"

She ran, the sound of the ripped soles of her footwear slapping on the cobblestones contrasting with the heavy thud of the officer's boots. She darted into a side alleyway, pushing past a surprised looking bum who had been squatting there and pushing one of the rubbish bins nearby over. Margaret's breath was rushing out of her in quick gasps, feeling numb to the chill of her drenched clothing pressing against her skin as the adrenaline coursing through her drove her to escape. *I have to get away. If he catches me now, everything I have worked to do until now will be worthless!*

She darted around another corner and found herself back by the Westminster Bridge, racing under the nearby bridge and pressed herself close to the wall, using the blanket that was draped over her shoulders to help her blend in to the stone around her. She held her hand over her mouth, doing her best to take deep, slow breaths while staying as quiet as possible. She could hear the sound of the officer's boots echoing menacingly off the cobblestones, but he still sounded far away. She heard him curse, the sound of his footsteps retreating into the night following shortly after.

"You hiding from them too?" A weary voice spoke up from the darkness behind her, causing her to gasp and whirl around on the spot. "We hide here because they don't like to bother coming under the bridges. I think they are afraid that we'll gang up on them and beat them to death or something like that. Not that they would be far off. Not like I hold particularly kind sentiments toward those stooges in uniform."

"What?" Margaret hadn't expected anyone else to be beneath the bridge, pushing her wet hair away from her eyes so that she could see. She found herself looking at five other people, the small group apparently having been watching her ever since she had darted beneath the bridge. She had been so preoccupied with escaping the officer that she hadn't even noticed any of them. "I'm sorry, I didn't realize this place was already taken."

She could just barely make out some of the features of the miserably huddled group. She could see two women and three men, all of whom shared a similar downcast expression. Their eyes were dull and lifeless, many of them doubling over with harsh bouts of coughing that lasted for minutes at a time. Margaret put her blanket absently over her mouth, keeping her distance from them. *They are all sick.*

"We fled here because we had nowhere else to go." It was a balding man whose front row of teeth were missing entirely that was talking to her. He was dressed in the dirty remnants of a monk's habit.

"What brought you here?" Margaret asked him.

"I was a fan of the drink, and I was a lover of betting. Those two things simply never play well, and I found myself having lost all my worldly possessions over a few ill-fated games of Euchre. I knew I should have just stuck to poker," he added jokingly, his face growing solemn surprisingly quickly. "Or maybe I should have just listened to my father's advice and joined the church. It is only now that I am laid at my lowest that I realize just how fortunate I truly was before."

"I wish I could say that my personal circumstances were caused by my own devices, but life has not been nearly that kind. I have been driven from place to place by desperation and my severe lack of a place to belong to. There was a place where I was beginning to get comfortable, but it turned out that my hopes for a lasting home there were fleeting at best," Margaret said, clenching her hands into fists. *I can't stay here. I don't wish to catch whatever it is they have, and...*

As Margaret took a step backwards, her foot slipped on the wet cobblestones. She felt her feet fall out from under her, and she grunted as her back hit the ground hard. She scrambled to get any grip, but her body slid down, and she felt the wind rush past her as she fell. The sunken eyes of the bald man were the last thing she saw before she was in free fall. Her mind flashed to the letter that was still nestled in her underclothes, dread filling her. *If I lose the letter, how will I ever be capable of clearing my name?*

The speed with which she hit the water drove the air from her lungs, her arms flailing to try and claw herself back toward the surface. Her chest burned as she broke the surface, gasping for breath while struggling to remain afloat.

The water was so cold. Freezing. She could even feel where sheets of ice had started to form, and they cracked and crunched against her arms as she fought to keep her head above the water.

"Help!" Margaret cried, the depth of the river making it so that she would have no hope of reaching the bottom while keeping her head above. She had never been a particularly strong swimmer, and the constant churning of the waters by the ships that navigated the river around her was making it even harder on her. "I can't swim!"

Margaret began to sob gently in the water at what seemed to be the arrival of her death. It hadn't come from starving or freezing to death of cold; instead, she was going to drown. She would die alone without ever clearing her name, and her promise to Ruth would die with her. *Maybe it's better this way. I'll be with Ruth again, and I won't have to worry about money or food or people trying to take advantage of me. I could see Mama again too.*

"There's a girl in the water! Lads, get me a rope!" came another voice from behind her, breaking Margaret out of her thoughts. She slowly tried to turn herself, the light of many lanterns helping her make out the ship that was approaching her. It was little more than a dinghy built to hold eight people at most, and Margaret could only make out three shadows. She felt water spray up into her face as something struck the water next to her, having the frame of mind to wrap her hands around the corded rope with as much strength as her half-frozen muscles could muster.

"Pull!" cried out the voice once more, a strong tugging sensation traveling down the rope as the men on the boat slowly began to pull her toward the boat. Margaret wished that she could offer some kind of assistance, but her teeth were chattering so powerfully that it was practically all she could hear. Her entire body felt as though it had been submerged in ice, and a chill was setting in within her that she feared might never be removed. "Almost got you now, madam. No need to worry!"

That voice; I've never heard it before, yet it seems so familiar to me. Strong hands reached down from the side of the boat and effortlessly seemed to pluck her from the river, water streaming from her clothing as she was set onto the wooden deck. Hands gently but insistently tugged the soaked blanket hanging from Margaret's shoulders off and flung it away, the wet slap of the fabric audible as it hit the wooden floor nearby. The same voice she had heard call for her to be aided now came from close beside her. "Let's get you out of these wet clothes into something warm."

Struggling to rise to her feet, Margaret raised her gaze to meet the eyes of her rescuer. He was a red haired young man in a smart brown suit, a pair of spectacles perched on the bridge of his nose that did nothing to hide his glittering green eyes. *I think I've seen him before. In fact, I'm almost certain I have.*

"That is a very interesting birthmark you have on your cheek," he whispered, his voice just loud enough for Margaret to hear. "I don't think anyone else in the world has a mark as distinct as that one. Are you the one that the bobbies have been talking about?"

"I didn't do it!" she blurted, her entire body shaking. "I would never do such a terrible thing. I was framed by that horrible woman because she couldn't stand someone as poor as me getting along with someone like Ruth. If I could change anything I've done, I would return to when Winifred was first scheming against me and put a stop to it. I would have quit, or insist that Ruth write her brother and see if I could just go work for him. She was my best friend!"

Her tears flowed down her cheeks unbidden, the accumulated grief from both the deaths of her father and

Ruth finally proving to be too much to contain. She collapsed onto the deck of the ship, her wails of despair echoing out across the water. She couldn't think, she couldn't speak; she could only kneel there until she felt a pair of arms gently wrapping around her. She hadn't noticed when the stranger had gotten close to her, but the change she felt was immediate.

Something about his presence caused peace to flow through her. After spending so many years being used to maintaining emotional walls, Margaret was finding all of her hard work being undone by a man that she only had a vague inkling that she should know. *He probably thinks I'm crazy.*

"You know, ever since I read the story in the papers, I asked myself if there was any chance they were true. I knew about you from what my sister wrote, and she never led me to believe that you were trying to use her for her money like so many of her so-called friends before you. The way she spoke of you as if you were our own flesh and blood, the excitement that I could sense through her letters when she recounted stories to me. I knew it would require a very special person to be able to evoke such a sensation from Ruth, especially when her letters up until then had been quite clear about her disdain for the other snobby girls at that school," he said softly.

"It can't be," Margaret's words were barely more than a whisper, her vision blurred as she gazed closer at his face. It all came in a rush of clarity; he was Timothy. His face looked familiar because it was the face she had seen in the picture Ruth had given her. "Timothy?"

"My sister was spot on when she said you were quick on the draw," Timothy replied with a laugh, his hand moving to gently push a few locks of her soaking wet hair away from her face. "But yes, I am Timothy Braddock. You must be Meg."

"Are you going to turn me in?" Meg asked, knowing that she didn't have the strength to run anymore regardless of his answer.

"No, Meg. I won't turn you in for a crime that I don't believe you committed. If anything, I have come to help you try and clear your name. I happen to have a letter from Ruth that has long since convinced me of your innocence, and I am sure that any judge worth their gavel will know when they've been had. I imagine that Winifred is going to have a very bad time in the coming months. Those are matters that we shall have to attend to in due time. Until then, relax and make yourself comfortable. You are amongst a friend now, Meg, and you don't have to live your life in fear anymore. You are safe," Timothy whispered.

CHAPTER 14

Time passed in a haze, Margaret's brain having trouble comprehending exactly what was going on. After she was fished out of the cold waters of the Thames, she had been ushered to a small private room where she could slip into fresh clean clothing. She was grieved to find that the letter was ruined beyond repair, with the parchment itself brittle and damp and the ink running until all legibility was lost. The picture of Timothy had fared better, but only a little. She'd been relieved to find herself in new clothing, but that had been only the beginning.

She found herself being hurried into an horse-drawn carriage by Timothy, who was adamant about remaining with her. The brief ride was pleasant, but all the while Margaret couldn't help worrying that this was all a ruse and she was about to be arrested. Timothy didn't speak much, but he did continue to offer her gentle smiles that helped put her mind a little more at ease. The gentle rocking of the carriage was soothing, and she found herself briefly dozing off as the accumulated exhaustion started to catch up with her. She awoke to Timothy gently shaking her, the young gentleman's warm smile still not having left his face. "Come along, we're nearly there."

Margaret gasped in amazement as she was led through the tall wooden doors of the manor house they'd arrived at, her shoeless feet padding softly on the wooden floors. She felt incredibly self conscious about the dirtiness of her feet, doing her best to walk on her tiptoes to limit the amount of grime she was tracking across the floor. Everything she could see, from the intricate etched designs on the stairwell railings to the pristine polish of the wooden surfaces, were testament to the wealth and cleanliness that were so prided by the family. She spotted a grand piano in a nearby room, the large instrument partially obstructed by the half-opened door to the room.

She was led up the stairwell and down a long hallway lined with portraits of Timothy and Ruth's ancestors, each looking more prim and proper than the last. Timothy narrated for her as they walked, giving her a little of the backstory about their family. They had been the family of former royalty whose wealth ended up being squandered by one of their less shrewd ancestors, resulting in the loss of the lands that they had owned for over a hundred years. They would have been doomed to poverty forever had it not been for Timothy's great great-grandfather, who had managed to win partial ownership of one of the smaller shipping companies and used his knowledge and luck to grow his business. "Nowadays, our shipping company is one of the biggest in the world, and we have an accountant who is responsible for verifying each of our transactions to ensure that nothing is slipping through the cracks that shouldn't. I'm happy to say that we haven't had any problems with embezzled funds, and with the careful spending practices my father instilled in me, I should be able to live comfortably for a very long time."

He came to a stop in front of a door with a spade etched on top, fishing a key from his pocket and pushing it into the lock. The faint click was lost to the sound of the door creaking open, causing Timothy to wince gently. "Sorry for the hinges. This room hasn't been used in a while, so I guess the servants have been slacking on maintaining it."

"It's okay," Margaret said, slowly stepping into the bedroom. In comparison to the rest of the manor, this room seemed remarkably bare. A large four poster bed that occupied over one-quarter of the room immediately drew Margaret's attention. It was covered in pink and white floral patterned bedding, a small teddy bear resting on a shelf that was mounted just above the headboard. A golden cuckoo clock that hung on the wall chimed, the little golden bird popping in and out of the doorway on top three times before vanishing back within. "Was this Ruth's room?"

"It was, and I hope it doesn't make you uncomfortable to be in here. I just need to ask you a few questions," he said softly, gesturing toward the bed. "Feel free to make yourself at home. If you require food or drink, I can send for something from the kitchen. I can imagine you haven't been enjoying much in terms of either for the last few weeks."

Margaret gently sat down on the bed, marveling at the springiness of the mattress. It seemed to cradle her body weight, giving her a sensation similar to what she thought sitting on a cloud might feel like. "I wouldn't mind something to eat or drink, but I fear that with how tired I feel I won't be able to stay awake long enough for anything to be prepared."

"That's fair. I'll try to have something prepared when you awake next," Timothy said, his eyes never leaving her. He seemed to be thinking intently, his gaze causing her to shiver slightly. The difference in the way that he looked at her compared to how the other men she'd encountered looked at her was stark. He seemed more worried about her well-being than anything else, even while she was on the run for having supposedly killed his sister. "You know, I've thought for a long time about what I would say to you when I first got the chance to meet you."

"How do you mean?" Margaret asked, reclining back against the many over fluffed pillows that populated the bed.

"Ruth always wrote about you in her letters since the day you arrived in that school and she saw you for the first time. She always lamented to me about how you seemed to constantly be the object of everyone's aggression, even though you seemed to be doing nothing more than your best to complete your duties. She described you to me, even down to the birthmark on your cheek. I could have sketched you in my sleep, and admittedly may have done so on more than one occasion to satisfy my own curiosity," Timothy admitted, running a hand through his red hair with a bashful smile.

Margaret blushed goodnaturedly at his confession but didn't interrupt. The thought that she had been so on his mind was one that she found awfully sweet. Ruth had apparently been talking her up to Timothy unbeknownst to her. *It is probably the only saving grace that I have at this moment. If he is willing to believe me over Winifred, then I still have hope.*

"When she wrote me a few weeks ago telling me that she was beginning to feel ill, I quickly made preparations to return back to London. I had hoped I would be able to return in time to send a doctor to the school, but whatever illness she had must have ravaged her frail body beyond repair. She always had a weak constitution; it was half of the reason why my parents were so adamant about the cleanliness of our home. With my father being a doctor, he knew all about the havoc that germs could wreak on a girl with a very weak immune system. She said that in the event something should happen to her, she wanted me to ensure you were looked after. That is why she wanted me to come back to town. So I could start the paperwork for our trust fund," he said.

"What trust fund?" Margaret asked, the cluelessness on her face helping to satisfy Timothy's doubts.

"My father, bless his soul, left behind a fund in his will for the two of us. It was originally to be given to the charge of the school, with the assumption that Ruth would be there and they would be able to see to it that her needs were met. However, he also stated that Ruth and I were the ones who remained in control of the money, and could choose to make other arrangements with the money if we so wished," Timothy said, his arms crossing gently across his chest. "Ruth had been telling me that she wished to offer you her half of the fund, which would ensure that you could continue on in her absence."

"It all makes sense now," Margaret whispered, her heart sinking. "Ruth must have told Winifred what her intentions were, and rather than allowing the money to slip through her fingers, Winifred made it look like I killed Ruth."

"What makes you so certain?" Timothy asked, a grave look on his face. "These are very serious accusations, after all."

"I was in your sister's room with her on the night she passed away. She confided in me before she died that the food she had been served for the three days prior had tasted off compared to usual. She said they all had an incredibly bitter taste compared to anything she'd ever had before, but had assumed it was just burnt seasonings," Margaret confided, her hands clutching at the blankets. "I never would have thought Winifred would stoop so low just to hold onto money that wasn't hers to begin with."

"I am sorry that I didn't intervene sooner," Timothy muttered, slowly rising from the bed and walking over to the large window that gazed out onto the garden behind the house. "I had harboured suspicions about Winifred from the first day that our mother and I dropped Ruth off at the school. There was something ugly in her eyes, like a beast that was waiting for its prey to drop its guard so it could be eaten. It is hard for me to believe that the headmistress of such a reputable school would ever do such a thing, but judging from what you've told me, it would make sense."

"What are we going to do now?" Margaret asked, biting her bottom lip. "I still can't show my face in town because the bobbies are all out looking for me. I nearly got captured by one earlier today when I was near the Westminster Bridge, and I am in no hurry to repeat that incident."

"You need have no fears, Meg. I promised my beloved sister that I would take care of you, and I have never been a man who would break his promise. Especially not to her," he added softly, his eyes moving in the direction of a picture of Ruth that hung on the far opposite wall. "I will go to the police at once and inform them that I have on good authority that the girl they are searching for has been framed. I shall be certain that their attentions are turned toward the true culprit, and that she is dealt with accordingly."

He returned to the bed and sat down next to her, causing her to squeak slightly when she felt his arms wrap around her. She blinked when she felt her head pressed gently against his firm chest, the gentle patting of his hand along the top of her back awfully soothing. Her breath hitched in her throat, eyes brimming with tears. *Can it really be that easy? Will I truly be able to walk around in daylight once more without fear?*

"Now that you are within these walls, think of them as your own personal castle. You are the princess now, and I your loyal knight. That wicked witch may think that her evil plan has gone off without a hitch, but you and I shall show her. However, I've kept you awake long enough. Rest, and once you are sufficiently restored, we can discuss your future then. A future that is sure to be far brighter than your past," he assured her, giving her hand a gentle squeeze before rising to his feet. He tipped his hat in farewell, motioning to the bell on the bedside table. "If you require anything, simply ring the bell. I have business I must attend to, but I hope to see you at dinner. Until then, I'll bid you farewell."

CHAPTER 15

Margaret sighed in relief as she sat on the bench in the back garden eight months later, one of Timothy's books from University held tightly in her hand. When she had admitted her interest in birds, Timothy had spent an hour searching through the library for the book. Using her finger to keep track of her place, she closed the book so she could glance at the title once more. *A history of the birds of Ceyron; Ceyron is another name for Sri Lanka, if I remember right. Could they truly have this many different breeds of birds in their country? That doesn't seem possible.*

"I thought I would find you back here," Timothy called out, standing at the top of the stone steps that led down to the garden path proper. His hand was raised in a cheerful wave, and Margaret was eager to return it. Her heart skipped a beat as she watched him stride toward her, every bit of his movements done with elegance and purpose. She was beginning to understand Ruth's infatuation with her brother, who seemed nearly perfect. His kindness to her had been unlike anything she had ever felt. He'd put his travels on hold so that he could remain around her, basically putting himself at her beck and call.

"I thought that I would come and give you some good news," Timothy said, reaching into the inner pocket of his coat and fishing out a dull brown mailing envelope.

"What is it?" she asked, closing the book fully and slipping her finger out from between the crisp pages, her hands folded atop one another on top of the book.

"I will get into that in a moment, but first," he glanced down at the book in her hand and smiled widely. "Good; you decided to take a look at it after all? I had worried that the language in it might prove to be a little dry for you, but the pictures within alone are worth their weight in gold. Such wonderful sketches and diagrams carefully placed alongside wonderfully vivid descriptions; A bird lover could not ask for much more."

"Yes, it has been a wonderful read," she patted the top of the book, giggling softly. "I was rather worried when I saw how thick of a book it was, but after skipping the introduction I was okay."

"That was exactly what I did when I was told to go through it in University. My professor was quite angry with me because he'd helped the man who wrote it get it published, so he was rather proud of it. While it is a wonderful tome of ornithological knowledge, I couldn't help harboring the feeling that to admit it to him would result in such an inflated ego I wouldn't be able to stomach him for the whole semester. A man so full of himself for his own achievements needs to be humbled every now and then," Timothy replied, tapping the top of the book gently. "What's your favorite kind of bird?"

"That's easy; I love Robins," she said, glancing across the garden to where a few goldfinches were sitting together on a high branch, chirping to one another gently. "I'd be lying if I said the goldfinches haven't started growing on me, though."

"Seems like I always see at least a couple of them back here every day; It's been that way for as long as I can remember. There used to be more, but that's because Ruth would always leave a bunch of bird seed out for them. It was what she would do whenever she was stressed or feeling sad about something that had happened. She spent six months where she was out here every day; she'd spend hours sitting here talking to them as they ate around her. I think it comforted her to see them all, since Mother and Father instilled their love of birds in us, ever since we were young," Timothy was smiling but his gaze looked distant, getting lost in his own memories for a moment. Margaret reached over, allowing her hand to gently squeeze his hand.

"Thank you once again for your kindness, Timothy," she said softly, her gaze meeting his when his head turned in her direction. "I don't know what would have happened had you not found me when you did."

"The kindness I have shown is only fitting for one of the few who befriended my sister out of genuine desire for her companionship. I can't begin to describe to you the many multitudes of people who have tried to endear themselves to us once they discovered our legacy. Backstabbers and two-faced associates have been something that constantly hounded our steps, and it made both my sister and I relatively jaded. However, you seem different. I don't know all the conditions of your previous life, but I would certainly wish to learn more about you. Assuming you are comfortable telling me," Timothy said softly, his hand having moved to gently take hers, squeezing it gently. "I know we found each other after Christmas, but you truly do feel like just a slightly late Christmas miracle." He grinned.

Margaret looked away from him, doubt emerging in her mind. "Why? What makes me so special?"

Timothy breathed deeply through his nose, the sudden movement of his hand causing Margaret to flinch bodily. She gasped when she felt his hand on her face, but rather than striking her, he merely cupped her cheek gently in his open palm. When she opened her eyes again she saw the sadness on his face, the gleam in his eyes caused by many unshed tears. "You brought Ruth back to life, Meg. Even if you hadn't realized it, and even if she had never told you, she left it all in her letters to me. You helped put her mind at ease in a way that she hadn't experienced since our Mother and Father have passed. As a fellow orphan she probably gravitated toward you because she sensed a kindred spirit, someone who could understand the pain she felt because they were feeling that same pain."

Tears fell unbidden from Margaret's eyes, a faint smile on her lips as Timothy's thumb immediately moved to try and wipe them away. "She used to joke with me about how you and I would be married someday and then we'd finally be sisters for real," she admitted, blushing furiously. She had grown incredibly comfortable with Timothy in the time they spent together, the two finding that they shared many of the same hobbies. He had shown her a whole world of things that she had only ever thought she would experience in her dreams, and had asked for nothing in return. "I was afraid to admit it before, but lately I'm starting to feel more and more certain of my feelings. It might be foolish of me to think, but I think we could be good together."

"Strange of you to say," Timothy said softly, tilting her head upward gently so that she had no choice but to gaze deeply into his eyes. "I've been thinking the same thing myself."

His lips were pressed against hers before Margaret could say anything else. Rather than freezing up, she felt herself practically melting into his touch. His lips felt so soft, and the scent of his cologne was making her mind slightly foggy. She hadn't realized just how badly she'd been falling for him over the last few months; or maybe, she just hadn't wanted to believe it. "You stole a maiden's first kiss," she breathed, playfully tapping his chest with her pointer finger. "I hope you are ready to take responsibility."

"I've been waiting a long time to have the chance to offer it to you," Timothy whispered softly. "Will you be my wife?"

"How could I ever say no to my knight in shining armor?" Margaret asked, dropping the book she had been holding, onto the bench, as she rose up onto her knees, wrapping her arms around Timothy's shoulders in a tight hug. She felt his arms close instantly around her in return, nuzzling her head lightly into his chest. "What is in the envelope?" she asked finally, gazing up at him.

"I'll give it to you later," he promised, driving all thoughts from Margaret's mind as he leaned down for another kiss.

The celebration of their wedding was a small, private affair per Margaret's request. She sent an invitation to Sally at her family's bakery and, after a small amount of hesitation, sent a letter to Abigail back at Boynton's. She hadn't wanted to limit Timothy's capacity to invite guests, but he seemed to be of the impression that not many people needed to know their business. She agreed wholeheartedly; why should others have to know that they've decided to pledge themselves to one another? Why should she have to put on some grand show when all that mattered was the feelings they had that led them to making the choice to tie the knot?

She still agreed to have it done in the church, with a priest present to witness it. Timothy had spared no expense in getting her fitted for a dress, the fabric hanging off of Margaret's body in a way that initially had her quite self conscious. She thought that it made her look malnourished, a fear that she was quick to express to the seamstress making her dress. The compromise was that the front of the dress was tightened up a bit, and that helped ease Margaret's anxiety. Two weeks after he had popped the question they were walking down the stairs of the church, Margaret's heart feeling as though it may explode from sheer elation.

Their honeymoon in France was like living out a fairy tale, Margaret periodically pinching herself to make sure that she wasn't just imagining it. They visited the Louvre, where Margaret was introduced for the first time to genuine classical art. She'd never seen anything like it, the vibrant colors and scenes they depicted seeming as though they might leap off the canvas at any moment. It helped that Timothy was so knowledgeable, and she felt as though she could listen to him talk for hours. He was so wonderfully gentle-mannered with her, treating her with a reverence that she had never seen any man treat a woman before. He was her personal Prince Charming, proving his love for her every day by leaving little love letters for her or having fresh flowers delivered to her.

Although many may consider their union rushed, it was the one decision she had ever made in her life that she wasn't second guessing.

As she stood on the balcony outside the ballroom of the dance hall, enjoying the night air, she took a moment to silently thank God. *Heavenly Father who lives in heaven, thank you for everything you've done for me. Thank you for sending Ruth into my life, and for letting me experience true friendship. I pray that you have taken her up into your kingdom where she may live on forever in your wondrous company. I pray that you watch over Timothy and I, and that our love lasts for the rest of our lives. I won't ask for anything else if you can just grant me that.*

"How are you feeling, Mrs. Margaret Braddock?" Timothy asked as he stepped up behind her, his hands stroking idly along her waist as he pressed a kiss to her cheek.

"I still feel like I'll wake up at any moment; this is better than any dream I could have ever hoped to imagine," she replied, her hand sliding up along his chest as she played absently with the lapel of his jacket. "I keep worrying I'll wake up tomorrow and find myself back in that room under the stairs, or under a bridge."

"This is no dream, my dove. I don't know how I can assuage your doubts, but I'm willing to spend the rest of my life reassuring you," he said, pulling out a familiar looking brown envelope. "This might help toward that reassurance, though."

"What is it?" Margaret peered at it curiously, wondering what news the envelope might contain that could cause her husband to be smiling so widely.

"Winifred has finally been officially tried for poisoning Ruth, and she's been found guilty. Your name is officially cleared of all wrongdoings, and the entire London police force has called off the manhunt for you," he said, taking her hands and setting the letter gently into them. "You have a clean slate with which you can pursue whatever sort of life you wish."

"So long as I get to spend my life with you, darling, I don't care what the rest of life holds for me," Margaret replied with a smile, tugging him by the hand back toward the dance floor while tucking the letter back into her brassiere. It could wait for later; for now, she wanted to dance the night away with her husband. That was how she would celebrate finally being free.

CHAPTER 16

"You are the last person I thought would come to see me," Winifred said gruffly, her bloodshot eyes gazing at Margaret with loathing from the other side of the bars of her cell. The letter she'd received from Timothy during their honeymoon had been to notify her of Winifred's sentence and the date of her execution.

"I wanted to talk to you one last time. Call it my way of getting closure," Margaret replied, crossing her arms gently in front of her chest. "I see that the year you have been here has not done much for your complexion, Headmistress. Or could it be that this is how you always look when stripped of all the things you took for granted?"

""At least I had things to lose to begin with," Winifred spat, her nose wrinkling in Margaret's direction. "How have you managed to survive on the streets this long? I had figured you would have died with the rest of the rats."

"That always was your problem, Winifred. You could never see past where I came from, acting like my past was the only thing of consequence about me. You assumed because of my father's poor choices that I was just like him, and you treated me worse than the garbage that I spent so many nights burning behind the school for you. I took a single piece of bread and you beat me until my legs were covered with bruises, for no other reason than it gave you joy. You even went so far as to kill my best friend because you couldn't accept that in that dungeon of misery you have created there still remained a person who remembered how to be kind to others." Margaret replied.

"I may die, but you will still be in the same position you were. Eventually you will find yourself back on the streets, forced to eat from the bins just to survive. I won't be surprised if you die cold and alone in a gutter somewhere, and not even your fleas will mourn you!" Winifred cackled, the sound just as cruel as ever. "At least I won't have to worry about anything where I am going."

"You are wrong, and always shall be wrong. If anything, your murder of Ruth simply sped up my inevitable meeting with her brother. Even though we barely knew one another, he helped me to clean away the mud you flung upon my name and my honour. It was with his kind help that you now find yourself where you are. It's funny, because even with how horrible you were to me, I would have gladly given money to the school to help keep it open." Margaret said, shaking her head. "You murdered Ruth for nothing, and all you've gained from it is the loss of your own life."

"I would have gotten away with it if Bertha hadn't allowed you to escape. I had hoped you would expire from the winter chill, but I should have known it would be harder than that to kill a cockroach like you," Winifred said, leaning back on the uncomfortable straw mattress that served as her bed. "Now my beloved school will die, and all those girls who relied upon it for their education shall be left wanting."

"Actually, that was part of the reason I came today," Margaret replied, reaching into the small handbag she had brought with her and pulling out a piece of parchment. "I have here the deed to the school. Timothy was kind enough to go down to the city clerk and purchased it outright. With you having no next of kin and about to be executed, it was agreed that you wouldn't be needing it anymore. I wanted you to know that despite how terrible you were to me, I will ensure that the school continues on after you are gone. However, it will be completely transformed from the way you had it. I am hoping to make it a place where my daughter could someday attend without fear," she said softly, her hand reaching down to stroke over her swollen stomach.

"What did you say?" Winifred asked softly, confusion briefly flashing across her face.

"I am going to be donating a small portion of my inheritance to the school to help keep it running. However, I will be sure to enforce a strict no bullying policy. Any instances of mistreatment by anyone towards staff or student alike will be swiftly reprimanded. It will be the kind of place where the headmistress wouldn't even think of caning a student," Margaret couldn't keep the tone of bitterness from her voice, the memory of Winifred's merciless beating still fresh in her memory. There were still nights where her legs would cramp up should she rest on them the wrong way, but Timothy would always massage them for her until the pain would pass.

Winifred sneered, turning her head to face away from Margaret. "That money won't last forever. What are you going to do when you find yourself penniless once more? How long will it be until you steal another slice of bread and get beaten once more?"

"Someone very important to me has given me his solemn oath that I will never have to worry about such things ever again. He has proven himself to be a man of his word so far, and I can imagine no reason why he would choose to change that now. Despite your hateful words and constant belittlement of me, I found someone who genuinely loves me. Who loves me for me and never raises his voice or hands to me. He will see to it that both my child and I are well taken care of, have no fears of that."

Margaret's eyes remained fixated on Winifred, the old woman having gotten awfully quiet.

Loud footsteps echoed down the stone hallway, causing Margaret to glance away from Winifred for the briefest moment. Timothy was currently striding toward them, the warm smile he always wore faltering for just a moment as his gaze wandered from her to Winifred. "Are you just about done here, Darling? I wanted to head over to the family plot in the cemetery so we could pay our respects."

"Of course, Darling. I was just saying my goodbyes," Margaret replied, smiling lovingly toward her husband as she felt his arm wrap gently around her own. "Well, goodbye Winifred. Hopefully your meeting with the Lord will give you a brighter disposition in the next life. And one last thing… I couldn't do this alone, but with the grace of God I can…"

Winifred's eyebrows went up, almost mockingly. "What is it? Spit it out."

"I forgive you." Margaret finally managed to say. "I forgive you for all the pain you caused me and my friend. Goodbye, Miss Winifred. Merry Christmas."

Winifred's mouth hung open, and she was speechless as Margaret stood up.

Timothy glanced at Winifred one last time before gently tugging Margaret's arm. She started walking away from the cell, half expecting Winifred to make some snide comment as they departed. No such sound came, and the two made their way back to the carriage in relative silence. "I hope that she didn't say anything that upset you too greatly," he said sourly, his hand patting the top of hers gently.

"No, Darling. She had surprisingly little to say to me. She's far more occupied with the knowledge that tomorrow is her final day before she has to face her maker. She's probably trying to come to grips with it all. I know that all those times where I stood facing the possibility of death that I was not very talkative either. The only one you can really talk to in that moment is God, and you don't have to speak aloud to do that. Many prefer that, I think," Margaret replied sagely, shaking her head. She was sad that Winifred had brought herself to this point, but she'd be lying if she said it didn't also bring her relief. Despite how broken the old headmistress looked in that cell, she had been the one who only months earlier had gleefully locked Margaret in a closet and tried to pin a murder on her. Good feelings weren't exactly in high supply when it came to Margaret's feelings about the older woman.

CHAPTER 17

"Are you sure that you want to come to the cemetery with me? I know it isn't the most cheerful place, and it is very cold this winter. I believe the whole place is covered in snow," Timothy said, helping her step up into the carriage before climbing up himself, calling to the coachman to get it moving.

Reclining across the seat opposite Timothy on the large pillow he'd brought for her, she looked over at her husband. He was gazing out of the window back in the direction of London proper as they started heading back toward their countryside manor, the cemetery located roughly ten miles away from it. The forest that surrounded it was immaculately covered in snow, and small animals scuttled across the forest floor out of sight of the carriage as it approached, leaving their footprints in the freshly laid snow. Birds chirped gently in the trees, unperturbed by the steady clopping of hooves and the creak of the wheels.

"Is something troubling you, Timothy? You've been quiet ever since we left the jail," Margaret said, gently forcing herself to sit up. He blinked several times before looking back at her, his green eyes looking melancholic and lost.

"I'm sorry, sweetling. I guess I have been avoiding coming here for a while ever since the funeral. Part of me wanted to keep you from coming with me because I didn't want you to be overcome by the guilt of her death. I have been trying very hard to keep myself from succumbing to the same, and I have been keeping that from you," he looked apologetic as he moved over to sit beside her.

"I know that the memory of her death is still raw for us, but we need to try and get back to the point that we can talk about her again. I appreciate that you've been trying to spare my feelings, but we are never going to be able to be truly happy until we can talk about her again. Our hearts are never going to heal until we can confront our grief, and I for one would like to talk about my memories with her. Aside from the time I've gotten to spend with you, my time with her was the happiest of my life," Margaret spoke softly, her hand moving to stroke along the top of her husband's head lightly. He was reclining gently against her, his lips pressing gently against her neck in a series of affectionate kisses.

"You are right, of course," he admitted softly, his hand squeezing hers as the carriage began to slow down. "Looks like we are arriving. I have some fresh flowers in the back of the carriage that we can place on the grave, and some candles to light as well. It is only proper that we close this chapter of our lives the right way."

"Let's go say our goodbyes, then," Margaret whispered, taking a deep breath to steady herself. "Ruth has waited long enough."

I only hope that her spirit can forgive me for making her wait this long. We'll have to leave a good offering before we go. I wonder if I should have brought some of those chocolates she used to like. Maybe next time we come.

CHAPTER 18

The small tombstone that sat above Ruth's grave had been carved with the image of small cherubins holding harps in their pudgy little arms. Margaret found herself disturbed by the lifelike representations before her, the cherubs almost seeming to be alive within the stone. Ruth's name was etched into the stone in some of the neatest handwriting Margaret had ever seen, filling the young woman with awe at the sheer skill that the craftsman must have possessed to accomplish such a feat. "They look so real," she breathed, kneeling next to it and gently running her hand over the smoothly polished stone, pushing off the layer of snow that had gathered on the top of it.

"It was done by an old friend of Ruth and mine. He got a job as a stonemason's apprentice and eventually took over his master's business when the latter got too old. When he heard what happened to Ruth, he told me he would take care of the headstone. I asked him how much he would need for it, but he refused to discuss payment. He's a good man; I'll be sure to pay his kindness forward in the future," Timothy replied, taking the bouquet of flowers he had been holding and setting them down on the mound of dirt that covered Ruth's casket.

"You've never given me a bouquet of flowers like these before," she said playfully, giving her husband a half-hearted shove. "How come you don't get me flowers?"

"You've never told me what kind of flowers you like, and I wouldn't want to bring a random assortment on the off chance that you manage to be allergic to one of them. Back when I was twelve and Ruth was a mere eight years old, I tried to collect some wildflowers that grew in the field behind our home for her. Upon giving her the flowers, we discovered a short while later when she began to have problems breathing that she had an allergy to one of the flowers. When my father realized what had happened, he took the flowers away and burned them. Wasn't the best first experience when it came to giving flowers," he admitted with a laugh.

"I can understand that," she said with a smile, leaning over to give her husband a kiss on his cheek. "However, I am not allergic to roses. You could always get me some of those," she teased.

"I'll be sure to keep it in mind," he grinned, wrapping his

arm around her as she set her own bouquet of flowers down onto Ruth's grave as well.

She smiled in return before her gaze fell once more to Ruth's grave. "Hi Ruth, sorry it took so long to get here. We've been rather conflicted, your brother and I, when it came to you. I wanted to come see your grave immediately, since I couldn't be at the funeral, but Timothy didn't think I would be able to cope with the finality of it all. In a way, I can't blame him. Gazing at your tombstone right now is one of the hardest things I've ever had to do," she whispered sadly, a few stray tears leaking from the corner of her right eye down her cheek.

She felt Timothy's hand on her shoulder, her hand moving to rest on top of it. She gave it a gentle squeeze, grateful for his support. "You used to tell me that you viewed me like a sister, but guess what? Timothy and I actually got married; I'm your sister-in-law now! He's been treating me so well and I've never found myself so happy before. At least, not since you were still here with me."

"We'll be making a donation to the school in your name, Ruth, and we'll make sure that it becomes a safe place for every one of our students. No one will ever have to worry about being starved or beaten or poisoned ever again," Timothy promised solemnly, a single tear managing to leak down his cheek before he wiped it away hastily. "I promise that I'll keep taking care of Meg, as well. The Lord knows she wouldn't do well without a chaperone," he joked casually, grunting softly when Margaret smacked him in the ribs.

"What is that supposed to mean?" she huffed irritably, glaring at him and trying not to smile.

"Well, the last time that you were left to your own devices you ended up almost drowned. Add to that the fact that you were on the run for a murder you'd been framed for, and I would have to come to the conclusion that you require someone to help keep you out of trouble," he said, rubbing his ribs tenderly.

"That was before; I am no longer the defenseless young girl that you rescued from the Thames that night. You've taught me self-defense and how to use a pistol, which puts me ahead of a good number of other women that I know. I refuse to allow myself to be the damsel anymore," Margaret responded defiantly, crossing her arms in front of her chest as she pouted.

"I didn't mean to insult you, Meg. I just wanted Ruth to know that I plan to make good on my promise and watch over you. That's all," he said, patting the top of her hand placatingly.

"That better be all you mean," Margaret muttered, unable to stop the smile that spread across her face as she leaned over to give him another kiss. When their lips finally separated she glanced back at the tombstone. Her knees felt slightly sore from kneeling for so long, but temporary discomfort was a small price to pay for closure. After all this time it felt like she was talking to Ruth again. Even if her friend would be unable to answer her, Margaret had the feeling that her friend was watching over her from Heaven. "Darling, I just got a wonderful idea. If the child ends up being a girl, did you want to name her after Ruth? In a way, it will feel like she returned to us."

"Could we truly?" Timothy asked, cupping Margaret's hands gently in his. "I didn't want to ask such a thing of you because I was worried you would find it peculiar. However, if you are okay with it, I would have no objections. I know Ruth would be touched beyond words to know that you held her in high enough esteem to want to name your child after her."

"She was my guardian angel on Earth; I can think of no greater honour I can do for her. It pales in comparison to everything she has done for me, but I like to think it can help me toward making up the difference," Margaret answered cheerfully, squeezing her husband's hand gently in return.

They sat together at Ruth's grave for a while, the two telling Ruth about all the things she had missed in the last year. Timothy and Margaret were laughing far more than they thought they would be, a small part of them feeling as though she were right there with them. The wind whistled softly through the trees that surrounded the cemetery, the bare branches rustling like the whispers of a thousand voices.

The sun slowly beginning to sink below the tree line was their signal to go, the cold of the day slowly giving way to an even colder evening breeze. Margaret reached down to stroke gently over her stomach, feeling it gurgle gently in hunger and realizing that she hadn't eaten anything today. The anticipation of coming to visit Ruth's grave had served to rob Margaret of her appetite, but now that the knot of tension had slackened within her, her body was reminding her of its needs. "I hope that the cooks have prepared something lovely for dinner today."

"I told them what time we expected to be home; I imagine they are preparing our meal for us even as we speak," Timothy assured her, grunting softly as he pushed himself off the ground. Fastidiously brushing dirt and snow from the knees of his trousers, he then reached down to help Margaret rise to her feet. She accepted his help gratefully, her pregnancy at the point where her mobility was starting to become more limited.

"We're heading home now, Ruth, but don't you worry. I promise that it won't take another year for me to come visit again. I'll even bring you some of your favorite chocolate bon-bons from the market next time; I know how much you used to love those," Margaret said, her hand stroking gently over the top of Ruth's tombstone. "I won't waste this second chance you've given me. I'll make certain that I offer the same kind of help to the poor that you showed to me. If I could come from nothing and make something of myself, I don't think there is any reason why others shouldn't be able to as well. Merry Christmas, Ruth."

"Hear hear," Timothy replied with gusto, the pair walking hand in hand away from the grave plot back toward the carriage. The coachman was the one to help her into the carriage this time, bowing to her before making his way back to his seat. When Timothy had taken his place beside her and closed the carriage door, the audible crack of a whip could be heard. The horses whinnied in protest, the carriage lurching forward shortly afterward.

Margaret rested her head back against Timothy's chest, happily content to just spend the ride in his arms. She hummed softly, the tune belonging to the song that Ruth had professed to love so much. To her surprise, Timothy began to hum along gently with her. Their two voices harmonized rather well, the sound audible only to the two of them. She felt his hand moving to stroke along her belly gently, her eyes rising to meet his gaze.

The sheer love in the look he gave her made her squirm happily in his grasp, straining to lean up just far enough that she could peck his cheek with a quick kiss. "Penny for your thoughts?"

"I am just thinking about something that Father used to say to Ruth and I when we were children. I used to think that happy endings were limited to story books, but the time I've spent with you has made me far less cynical when it comes to love. I wake up each morning with you and I find myself looking forward to the day for no other reason than I get to spend it with you," Timothy admitted, watching a pair of robins fly past the window of the carriage, their merry chirping bringing a smile to the couple's lips. "Look darling; Your favorite bird is flying by. Ruth must be sending us a sign."

Definitely feels like a sign from her. God once sent a bird to tell Noah that he and his family were safe in the aftermath of the Flood; perhaps this is my version of the olive branch. "Does that mean that the rain of my life is over, and I have nothing but sunshine to look forward to?"

"As long as I live and breathe," Timothy replied after a moment, his voice just loud enough that Margaret could hear him. "I would cross the oceans of the world and try and retrieve the moon from the sky if it meant your continued happiness."

"Who would have guessed that you were such a romantic," she purred, her hand reaching up to gently stroke along his cheek. "Were you this charming to all the ladies?"

"Only you, my sweetling," Timothy answered immediately, sighing in relief as the Manor began to become visible in the distance. "Only you."

"I guess that makes me a very lucky woman," she replied, and she truly meant it. "I love you very much, Timothy."

"I love you more," he replied playfully, making her giggle softly.

"I love you most."

THANK YOU FOR CHOOSING A PUREREAD BOOK!

We hope you enjoyed the story, and as a way to thank you for choosing PureRead we'd like to send you this free book, and other fun reader rewards...

Click here for your free copy of Whitechapel Waif
PureRead.com/victorian

Thanks again for reading.
See you soon!

OTHER BOOKS BY JESS WEIR

If you loved this story why not read other books by the same author?

The Midwife's Dream

The Mill Daughter's Courage

The Orphan Pickpocket's Christmas

The Little London Nightingale

Printed in Great Britain
by Amazon